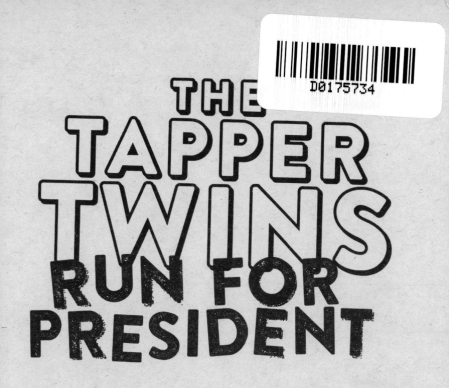

THE TAPPER TWINS RUN FOR PRESIDENT

MOB SCENE IN LIBRARY
(not actual mob) (but close)

skronkmonster MY NAME IS REESE TAPPER AND IM RUNNING FOR PRESIDANT!!!!!!

(spelling fail)

THE TAPPER TWINS RUN FOR PRESIDENT

Ugh. Fine. But when this blows up in our faces I will blame you

MOM
(on Reese's phone)

This is Reese's mother. The Supreme Court ruling does not apply to 12-year-olds. Please delete that entire page ASAP, or I will call YOUR mother

VOTE CLAUDIA TAPPER
(unintentional strangling)
FOR A BETTER TOMORROW

plate I threw at Reese's head
(not actual plate)
(b/c original one broke)

PLEASE PLEASE PLEASE DO NOT WRITE ABOUT THIS

GEOFF RODKEY

DAD → My whole body just clenched up in fear

SCHOLASTIC INC.

ISBN 978-1-338-13289-2

12 11 10 9 8 7 6 5 4 3 2 1 16 17 18 19 20 21

Printed in the U.S.A. 40

First Scholastic printing, September 2016

AN ORAL HISTORY OF
THE CULVERT PREP MIDDLE SCHOOL
SIXTH GRADE CLASS ELECTION
(Second Semester)

compiled from interviews conducted by

CLAUDIA TAPPER

with

a whole bunch of people, including:

CANDIDATES FOR PRESIDENT

Claudia Tapper

Reese Tapper

VOTE
REESE

James Mantolini

CANDIDATES FOR TREASURER

Carmen Gutierrez

Xander Billington

Max Esper

SENIOR CAMPAIGN STAFF

Akash Gupta

Kalisha Hendricks

MEDIA

Sophie Koh,

<u>The Culvert Chronicle</u>

SQUIRREL

Nutty the Squirrel*

*not actually interviewed

CONTENTS

PROLOGUE

CLAUDIA

My name is Claudia Tapper. I'm twelve years old. And I'm just going to be completely honest about this: I want to be president.

And not just president of the sixth grade, but the whole United States.

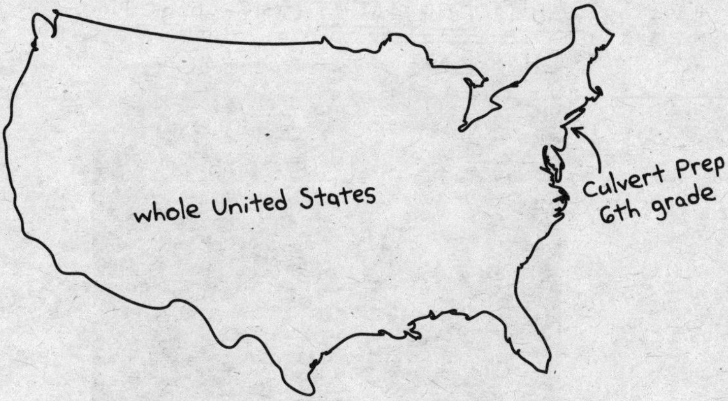

whole United States
Culvert Prep 6th grade

I know this probably sounds obnoxious. But I think it's very important to set big goals for yourself and try to be the best person you can be. That way, even if you fall short, you could still end up being vice president.

(I also want to be a famous singer-songwriter— but that is a whole other story)

or maybe governor of something

I also know getting elected president is a MAJOR long shot, and I'll have to face a ton of challenges to pull it off. For the record, I am totally fine with that. Facing big challenges and kicking butt at them is what makes a person a strong leader. Nobody wants a president who didn't have to work hard to get the job.

President Warren G. Harding (1921–23): didn't have to work v. hard to get job—WAS TERRIBLE AT IT (srsly—google him)

That's why I decided to put together this book, which is the official history of my campaign to be re-elected president of Culvert Prep's sixth grade class.

Because that election was the biggest challenge of my life.

Mostly thanks to my stupid twin brother.

REESE

I seriously was NOT planning to run for president.

I mean, it's not like I want to be one when I grow up. I've seen the real president on TV, and there's no way I'd want that guy's job. He spends his whole day wearing a suit and getting yelled at. It's even worse than being a lawyer.

not true. Dad is a lawyer— it is MUCH worse than being president

But the thing is, sometimes you have to stand up for your beliefs. And that's what I was doing.

This election wasn't about me.

It was about freedom.

Reese HAS NO CLUE what that even means (his campaign manager taught him to say it)

MOM AND DAD (Text messages copied from Dad's phone)

MOM →

FYI, Claudia's writing another oral history

oral history = my interviews w/everybody involved

DAD →

My whole body just clenched up in fear

I told her she can't use our texts this time

Smart move. We would look like worst parents ever

No kidding. Especially me

Just don't leave your phone lying around or she will steal it and take screenshots

Don't worry—my phone is password-protected

Dad's password=7734

CHAPTER 1
DOGGIE TERROR FROM THE SKIES

CLAUDIA

None of this ever would have happened if Reese hadn't almost murdered a very small dog with a soccer ball.

REESE

I did NOT almost murder it! The dog didn't even get hurt!

And it was a total accident! So even if I'd skronked the dog, it wouldn't have been murder. It would've been, like... dogslaughter.

not a real word

(like "manslaughter," but with dog?)
(either way, not a real word)

CLAUDIA

I should back up a little and explain the situation.

Reese and I live in New York City. Which is awesome. It's actually TOO awesome, because so many people want to live here that it is seriously overcrowded.

And it's not just overcrowded in the subway, or the grocery store, or Midtown during the holidays, but everywhere. There is just no space at all.

Midtown during holidays=INSANELY CROWDED

For example: size-wise, my bedroom is somewhere between a very tiny closet and a very large shoebox.

Not that I'm complaining. I'm actually very grateful I even HAVE a bedroom. If Reese and I had to share a room, it would be a total nightmare. For a LOT of reasons. But especially because he smells horrible.

REESE

Okay, THAT is not fair. I only smell bad after soccer.

CLAUDIA

Reese, you play soccer EVERY SINGLE DAY.

REESE

No way! I play, like, five days a week. Tops.

CLAUDIA

Okay, so—FIVE out of seven days, you smell like a butt...that's been stuffed inside a moldy shoe...with some rotten vegetables.

REESE

Yeah. But only five.

CLAUDIA

I am getting seriously off track here. My point is, New York City is SO overcrowded that sometimes normal things end up in not-normal places. Like our school's playground. Which, instead of being in a normal place—like next to the parking lot—is on the roof. Five stories up.

(also, there's no parking lot)

And if you are insane enough to get into a contest to see who can kick a soccer ball over the rooftop fence—

rooftop fence
(actually more of a wall)
(looks kind of like a prison)
(probably on purpose)

REESE

It wasn't a contest! It was a bet. And the bet was I couldn't do a bicycle kick from in front of the SOUTH fence that was high enough to clear the whole NORTH fence—which was ridic hard, 'cause it was January and I was wearing snow boots. So it's totally beast that I nailed it.

Now that I think of it, Xander still owes me five bucks for that.

CLAUDIA

Like I was saying: if you're insane enough to kick your soccer ball over the rooftop fence, New York City's SO overcrowded that even if you DON'T actually take out some mean rich lady's equally mean little dog while she's walking it down 77th Street...

MEAN RICH LADY/
MEAN LITTLE DOG

the ball will come screaming down out of the sky and scare BOTH the mean little dog AND the mean rich lady SO MUCH that she'll march into Culvert Prep and demand to talk to whoever's in charge of not letting soccer balls fly off the roof.

dog was very mean EVEN BEFORE this happened (so was owner)

And THAT is how Vice Principal Bevan wound up banning soccer from the roof.

REESE

Which was totally cray! That was, like, a straight-up attack on my freedom. And my liberty. And my human rights to, like, kick soccer balls during free time.

And that's why I got into politics.

srsly, Reese has NO CLUE what all these words even mean

CHAPTER 2
OUR APARTMENT HAS A SUPREME LEADER

(And Other Stuff You Should Know About Politics)

CLAUDIA

In case you're like my brother and have no idea what politics even is, it's all about who gets to decide the really important questions in a country and/or middle school. Like "Should soccer balls be banned from the roof?" Or "What if we invade Canada?"

There are a bunch of ways politics can work. But the two most common ones are "dictatorship" and "democracy."

(i.e., the dictator)

In a dictatorship, one person decides everything. Then everybody else has to do whatever that person says. It's VERY unfair.

Two good examples of dictatorships are North Korea and our apartment.

REESE

The dictator of our apartment is Mom. But she's pretty cool about it.

Dad not happy about this

CLAUDIA

It is definitely much better to live in our apartment than North Korea. For one thing, we have totally uncensored Internet access. Mostly because Mom couldn't figure out the parental control app.

Plus, she works crazy-long hours. So most of the time, Ashley, our after-school sitter, is the substitute dictator. And tbh, Ashley is a total pushover. For example, last year she let Reese eat nothing but Cheezy Puffs for dinner for three straight weeks.

(Dad's hours are even crazier/longer)

I am still a little surprised that didn't kill him.

Cheezy Puffs (will srsly kill you if you eat enough)

REESE

It ALMOST did. By the end, I think my skin was turning orange.

CLAUDIA

The second kind of politics is a democracy, where everybody gets to vote on all the important questions.

(U.S.A. population)

But in a country of 320,000,000 people—or even a sixth grade of 97 people—letting everybody vote on everything is way too complicated. So instead, everybody votes on who their leaders should be, and then the leaders make the decisions.

(FYI: this is called "representative" democracy)

REESE

So is school a dictatorship? Or a democracy? 'Cause we defs don't have uncensored Internet access. You can't get on ANY good sites from the cafeteria Wi-Fi.

CLAUDIA

Culvert Prep is a mix. It's basically 90% dictatorship and 10% democracy.

CULVERT PREP
(90% dictatorship)

(rooftop playground/prison
is over here)

REESE

Who's the dictator of Culvert Prep? Vice Principal Bevan?

CLAUDIA

No, it's the Head of School, Ms. Tingley. Plus Principal Spooner. Vice Principal Bevan's more like their army. Like, whenever there's rioting in the streets, they send her in to restore order.

REESE

I have no clue what you're talking about. All I know is, Mrs. Bevan's the one who banned soccer balls from the roof.

And when me and Xander and Wyatt were like, "Puhhhleeeeaase let us play soccer on the roof again!" she was all, "Why don't you ask your class rep to bring it up in SG?"

SG = Student Government

CLAUDIA

Student Government is the 10% democracy part of Culvert Prep Middle School. SG is made up of one representative (a "rep") from each homeroom class, plus a president and a treasurer for each grade.

The class rep for Reese's homeroom is my second-best friend Carmen.

tied with Parvati.
So, rank is:
1. Sophie
2. Carmen (tie)
2. Parvati (tie)

CARMEN GUTIERREZ, 6th grade class rep/second-best friend of Claudia

So your brother and his friends come up to me at lunch, and they're like, "You GOTTA get the SG to tell Mrs. Bevan to let us play soccer on the roof!"

But the thing is, I've been trying to get Culvert Prep to install solar panels on the roof FOR-EVER. Solar power's MAJOR for our future—if we don't stop burning coal and oil, the ice caps are going to melt, New York City's going to be totally underwater, and we're ALL GOING TO DROWN.

CLAUDIA

Carmen is VERY concerned about global warming. It's basically the whole reason she ran for class rep.

CARMEN

It's been ridic hard to get solar panels approved. Whenever I'd bring it up in SG, Mr. McDonald would be like, "There's just so much sports playing on the roof that I don't know if it's really practical."

Mr. McDonald = SG's faculty advisor

So I saw this soccer ban as a MAJOR opportunity. And I was like, "I'm sorry, Reese. The future of human civilization's at stake here."

And Reese was like, "So's our soccer game!"

So I said, "Maybe you should discuss it with someone else in SG."

And he was like, "Who?"

And I was like, "Duh! The class president."

CLAUDIA

And at that moment, the class president was me.

CHAPTER 3
MY POLITICAL CAREER (ALL SEVEN YEARS OF IT)

me: long career of devoted public service

CLAUDIA

Just so everybody understands how hard I worked to become sixth grade class president, here is a chart of my political career to date:

	GRADE	OFFICE	MAJOR ACCOMPLISHMENTS
Junior School	Kindergarten	Line leader	kept line straight
	1st	Tech cart monitor	wiped screens clean every week; no viruses found on ANY laptops while I was in office
	2nd	Green team	spearheaded new cloth napkin policy
	3rd	Book fair volunteer	created "design your own bookmark" craft table, staffed lemonade stand
	4th	Green team (again)	improved classroom recycling 75%; added yogurt containers to list of recyclables
Middle School	5th	President (2 terms)	added "dress as favorite book character" day to Spirit Week, increased bake sale revenue 200%, created & ran talent show
	6th	President (1 term SO FAR)	led drive for "zero tolerance" cyberbullying policy, organized charity scavenger hunt

As you can see, I've been in public service over half my life. I've tried VERY hard to make Culvert Prep and the world in general a better place. And I think I've done a pretty good job.

In fact, everyone's been so happy with the job I've done that in the last two elections, I mostly ran unopposed.

↑ elections are twice a year (Sept. and Jan.)

I say "mostly" because James Mantolini was also on the ballot both times. But I'm pretty sure he didn't get a single vote. Possibly not even from himself.

This is because James is out of his mind.

JAMES MANTOLINI, presidential candidate/ professional crazy person

I run for president to bring attention to issues that other candidates are too scared to talk about.

Like whether some of our teachers are secretly robots.

CLAUDIA

The Secret Robot Menace was James's big issue in the last election. It was so insane that I took a picture of one of his campaign posters just in case historians of the future didn't believe me.

ROBOTS:
DO THEY WALK AMONG US?
VOTE MANTOLINI.
HE'LL STOP THE ROBOTS.

The election before that, James's issue was "secession."

DICTIONARY

secession

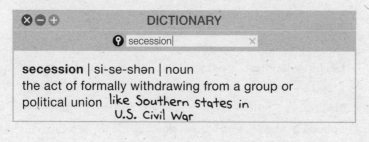

secession | si-se-shən | noun
the act of formally withdrawing from a group or political union like Southern states in U.S. Civil War

James wanted the fifth grade to "secede" from the rest of Culvert Prep. But pretty much no fifth grader on earth has ANY IDEA what that means. And his campaign posters did not exactly help.

SECESSION:
JUST BECAUSE YOU DON'T KNOW WHAT IT IS...
DOESN'T MEAN IT'S A BAD IDEA
5TH GRADE
CULVERT PREP
VOTE MANTOLINI
FOR A FREE AND INDEPENDENT 5TH GRADE

REESE

That whole se-so-se-whatchamacallit thing was just crazypants. When James finally explained what it was, we were like, "Wait...if the whole fifth grade quit the school, where would we go all day?"

And James was like, "Starbucks. If everybody orders a coffee, we can sit there as long as we want."

CLAUDIA

Even though secession was completely insane, in my campaign that year, I promised to study the issue to see if it was a good idea for the kids of the fifth grade. (IT WASN'T)

This is because I believe it's VERY important for a president to represent EVERYONE fairly and equally. Even people who are crazy and/or think it's cool to kick soccer balls off the roof.

Which is why, when Reese and his soccer idiot friends Xander and Wyatt came to me to complain about the roof situation, I listened.

REESE

No, you didn't! You just said you'd study the issue!

WYATT TEMPLEMAN, friend of Reese/ soccer idiot

Which totally meant you were going to blow us off!

XANDER BILLINGTON, friend of Reese/ soccer idiot (also huge idiot in general)

True dat! I's all, "Don't be frontin' dat skeezy ish wit us, Cruella da Prez! RATCHET!"

CLAUDIA

Speaking of words nobody understands, I should explain about Xander Billington. He's from a very old, very rich, and very brain-dead family. Xander's great-great-great-great-whatever-grandfather Billington came to America on the *Mayflower* with the original Pilgrims.

This was probably very annoying for the other Pilgrims.

AWW YEAH, INDIANZ! BILLINGTON BRINGIN' DA JAMZ!
Billington! They're NOT Indians! They're Native Americans!
This is SO embarrassing.
THE LANDING OF THE PILGRIMS AT PLYMOUTH. MASS. DEC. 22ND 1620.

When Xander started dissing me like we were in a rap battle, I stayed classy. Instead of calling all of them names, too, I said, "If you don't like the way I'm representing you as president, there's an election coming up."

What I meant by that was, "You should vote against me."

What I did NOT mean by that was, "You should run for president yourself."

Unfortunately, I did not make this clear to Reese.

CHAPTER 4
REESE'S POLITICAL CAREER (ALL TWO MINUTES OF IT)

my brother:
long career of
sitting on couch
shooting zombies

XANDER

At first, I was all, "Yo, I should straight-up run for president! I'ma stone cold RULE dis hizz-ouse!"

REESE

Wyatt and I were like, "Ummm...maaaaaybe."

Because we didn't want to make Xander feel bad. But it seemed, like, not possible for him to win an election.

WYATT

The thing is, Reese and I are totally cool with Xander. But a lot of people basically hate him. ← true also true

People really DO like Reese, though. Because he's super-nice to everybody. So I was like, "What if REESE runs for president?"

EXCEPT HIS SISTER

XANDER

First, I's all, "Wuuuuut?"

But then I's all, "Aaaaite. I'ma HAMMER DOWN on dem treasurer doe." 'Cause then I be rollin' in dem Benjamins.

BENJAMINS = $100 BILLS (had to draw this b/c couldn't get pic of real one)

THE UNITED STATES OF AMERICA
100
KB46279860I
ONE HUNDRED DOLLARS

(Benjamin Franklin) (obvs)

REESE

So Wyatt and Xander wanted me to run for president, Xander for treasurer, and Wyatt for class rep.

Which seemed like a TON of work just to play soccer on the roof.

Plus part of me was like, "I think Claudia might get mad if I ran against her."

OH, REALLY? DO YOU THINK???

So that night while Ashley was making us dinner, I asked Claudia what she thought of me running for president.

And she laughed at me. Like, hard. For a really long time.

CLAUDIA

I did NOT laugh at him.

ASHLEY O'ROURKE, after-school sitter/ substitute dictator

Ohmygosh, Claude, you TOTALLY laughed at him! You were like, "Reese, the ONLY way you could win is if an asteroid hit Manhattan and killed everybody else who was running. Plus all the voters."

Then you both got all up in each other's business, and I had to jump in and break it up, and I couldn't focus on making dinner, so I totally burned the chicken.

ASHLEY = not good at focusing while making dinner

DINNER (burning)
NOT DINNER

CLAUDIA

Okay, fine. I laughed at him. But here's why:

Student Government is MY thing, the same way soccer is REESE'S thing. And right up until then, Reese felt the same way about SG that I felt about soccer—that it was totally pointless, he could care less about it, and he had no clue how it worked.

So for him to suddenly decide to run for president was not only completely insane, but also very mean and hurtful to me personally.

But it's not like I was going to tell Reese that.

So instead, I laughed at him.

Because it was ALSO totally hilarious. Reese trying to be president was like me running onto his soccer field in the middle of a game and trying to play ~~quarterback~~: goalie (whatever) the funniest thing ever for anybody watching, but a total fail for Reese (as president) and/or me (as ~~quarterback~~ goalie).

For the record, when I went on ClickChat after dinner and told my friends, they thought it was hilarious, too.

CLICKCHAT POSTS (PRIVATE CHAT)

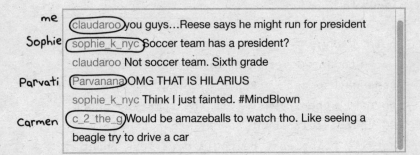

me — claudaroo you guys...Reese says he might run for president

Sophie — sophie_k_nyc Soccer team has a president?

claudaroo Not soccer team. Sixth grade

Parvati — Parvanana OMG THAT IS HILARIUS

sophie_k_nyc Think I just fainted. #MindBlown

Carmen — c_2_the_g Would be amazeballs to watch tho. Like seeing a beagle try to drive a car

CLAUDIA

But since part of being a leader is admitting your mistakes, I will admit that laughing at Reese was a huge mistake. Because my brother is INSANELY competitive. He's so competitive that once when I beat him at checkers, he went nuts and tried to eat the checkers.

REESE

I totally shouldn't have done that. Turns out you can't chew that kind of plastic without seriously hurting your mouth.

WARNING: DO NOT EAT

CLAUDIA

So making fun of Reese for wanting to be president was like waving a red flag in front of a bull.

REESE

I got seriously spun out. Like, whenever Claudia tells me she can kick my butt at something, it just gets me twice as hyped to kick HER butt. So when she laughed at me, all I wanted to do was just pwn her, BAD. actually a word (google it)

I got so hyped that right after dinner, I posted on ClickChat that I was running.

CLICKCHAT STATUS UPDATE FOR REESE TAPPER

skronkmonster MY NAME IS REESE TAPPER AND IM RUNNING FOR PRESIDANT!!!!!!

(spelling fail)

REESE

Then I figured I should, like, get in shape for the election. So I got out my iPad and used the voice memo app to record myself going, "MY NAME IS REESE TAPPER, AND I'M RUNNING FOR PRESIDENT." Because I knew from this movie I saw that people say that a lot when they're running. And I wanted to sound totally beast.

But when I listened to it, my voice was all squeaky and stuff. I was like, "Oh, man—do I really sound like that?"

I was about to record it again when Claudia busted in and went off on me.

CLAUDIA

It's important to note here that when I saw Reese's ClickChat post, I got very upset.

Because I CARE A LOT about Student Government. I take it very seriously, and I've worked very hard at it. For years.

And Reese DIDN'T care about SG, didn't take it seriously, and doesn't work hard at ANYTHING. (Except video games. And maybe soccer.)

So him running against me was really upsetting. In fact, it was so upsetting it made me cry.

For a minute.

And then I got angry. Very angry.

And I think all of us, when we are angry like that, say things that are kind of crazy and/or we don't really mean. Especially when we're having a big fight with our brother in the privacy of our own home and have NO IDEA HE'S SECRETLY RECORDING IT.

REESE

I wasn't recording it on purpose! It was a total accident!

But, like...yeah. The voice memo app was on. So when Claudia came in and went off on me, I accidentally recorded her exact words.

TRANSCRIPT OF RECORDING REESE SECRETLY MADE OF CLAUDIA

Oh, hey, Reese? FYI?

I'm going to DESTROY YOU! I will GRIND YOUR BONES INTO DUST!

The only election you're going to win is "MOST LIKELY TO GET HIS BUTT KICKED!"

And when I'm re-elected? In a LANDSLIDE? I will devote my ENTIRE presidency to WIPING SOCCER OFF THE MAP!

When I'm done, you won't even be able to play it in gym class! You'll get suspended just for talking about it at lunch! I'll get soccer jerseys banned like yoga pants were! And you and every DROOLING IDIOT who ever kicked a soccer ball at Culvert Prep will BEG ME FOR MERCY!

And I will hear your cries.

And I will laugh at them.

Good luck with your campaign.

CLAUDIA

Like I said, I was very angry. And hurt. And upset. And I obviously DID NOT MEAN anything I said. I was just trying to scare my brother.

Which, BTW? Mission accomplished.

artist's re-creation of what Reese looked like after I scared him (P.S.—artist is me)

REESE

I was definitely scared. Because Claudia was FIERCE.

Plus she sounded super-presidential. Like, her voice wasn't squeaky AT ALL.

So I started thinking, "Oh, man... maybe I should delete that ClickChat post and forget the whole thing."

But then she got Mom and Dad involved. Which was TOTALLY NOT COOL.

CHAPTER 5
I SHOULD NOT HAVE GOTTEN MOM AND DAD INVOLVED

EDITOR'S NOTE: FYI, editor is me

Mom and Dad think this chapter is totally unfair and inaccurate.

But Reese and I think it's COMPLETELY fair and accurate. So I left it in.

But I did write "M.D.U." (for "Mom Dad Unfair") next to everything they complained about.

CLAUDIA

If I had it to do over again, I would NOT have called Mom to complain about Reese running for president. Even though it was totally mean and hurtful of him, I should've just handled it myself.

Here's why:

When something bad happens around our apartment, 90% of the time it's Reese's fault. And since Mom and Dad work crazy-long hours and don't have much time to get involved in stuff,

M.D.U.

M.D.U.

bad stuff includes:
- busted furniture
- food left in strange places (see pic)
- walking through apt. w/dog poop on shoes

when they DO get involved, 100% of the time they yell at Reese first. M.D.U.

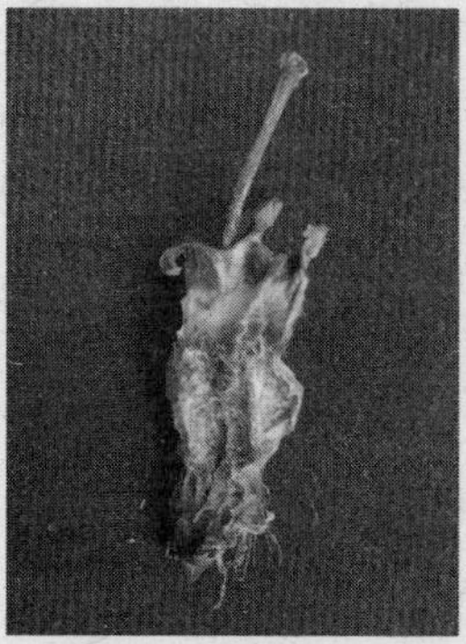

FOUND UNDER COUCH CUSHIONS
(was there at least 2 weeks)
(Reese's fault)

It's just easier that way. And 90% of the time, it makes total sense.

BUT if you do the math, this means 10% of the time, Reese is getting yelled at for stuff that's not totally his fault. M.D.U.

It happens often enough that Reese has a major complex about it. So whenever Mom and Dad get mad at him—EVEN when it's all his fault—Reese gets totally defensive and throws a huge fit about how everybody always blames him for everything, and nobody's ever on his side, and the whole family's ganging up on him.

I'm not saying he doesn't have a point. But he gets way too emotional.

And when he blows up like that, Mom and Dad either [A) get three times as mad at him, B) feel totally guilty about getting mad at him in the first place, C) overcompensate by turning around and yelling at ME, or D) all of the above.] M.D.U.

And what happened here was a D).

MOM AND DAD (text messages)

Claudia called—Reese running against her for class president

OMG CALLING YOU NOW

Can't talk on phone yelling at Reese

M.D.U. (M says she was "exaggerating" and "not really yelling")

REESE

Mom called me from work and was like, "Reese, you can't do this to your sister!"

And I totally went off. I was like, "WHAT ABOUT WHAT SHE'S DOING TO ME? ALL WE WANTED WAS TO PLAY SOCCER ON THE ROOF AND

SHE BLEW US OFF AND LAUGHED AT ME AND NOW I HAVE TO PWN HER AND IT'S ALL HER FAULT AND I CAN'T BELIEVE YOU'RE TAKING HER SIDE AND THIS IS TOTALLY UNFAIR!"

CLAUDIA

While Reese was having a meltdown with Mom, Dad called me to get my side of the story.

By then, I'd realized getting Mom involved was a mistake. Because it pretty much guaranteed Reese would go nuts and fight me to the death.

So I told Dad I could handle it myself, and he should tell Mom that ASAP.

MOM AND DAD (text messages)

Claudia says it's fine. Call me

Can't. Still on with Reese. He is playing victim card

M.D.U. (M claims "just kidding")

REESE

Mom was like, "You can't run for president! End of story!"

And I was like, "THIS IS SO SKRONKING UNFAIR!!!! YOU ALWAYS TAKE CLAUDIA'S SIDE! THIS WHOLE FAMILY'S AGAINST ME!!!"

Then I called Dad.

CLAUDIA

While Reese was on with Dad, Mom called me again. And she must have been feeling major guilt about yelling at Reese, because she did a complete 180 and started yelling at me instead. M.D.U. (M claims she was not yelling) (but she was)

It was a lot of drama.

MOM AND DAD (text messages)

Srsly cannot believe our kids

Also I am worst parent on earth

Feel terrible I lost my temper

Don't think we can forbid Reese from running

You missed the part where you tell me I am not worst parent on earth

YOU ARE GREAT MOM! And wife! And businesswoman! You can plan my castle onslaught any day

Princess Bride reference (Dad's favorite movie) (P.S. it is awesome—check it out)

Whatever. Think we should tell Reese he can't run, then tell Claudia she has to help him w/soccer roof thing

Not sure. What about our new parenting style?

Kind but firm? That's what I'm doing

Except I forgot the kind part

No the other one. Let them make mistakes

??? That is dumbest thing I ever heard

It was your idea

Not ringing a bell

Sunday NYT article. You emailed me link. Said it was brilliant

Hang on let me reread article

Ugh. Fine. But when this blows up in our faces I will blame you

ENTIRE TEXT EXCHANGE = MDU

(both say they were "just joking around" and "didn't mean any of it")

VOTE CLAUDIA

CHAPTER 6
CAMPAIGN KICKOFFS (AND POSTER PROBLEMS)

CLAUDIA

Reese and his running mates (Xander and Wyatt) kicked off their campaign with a whole bunch of bad ideas. Like creating a campaign headquarters on MetaWorld.

REESE

I have this totally beast castle on the Planet Amigo server, and we turned it into Election Central. Then we gave out free titanium armor to everybody who said they'd vote for me.

REESE'S "ELECTION CENTRAL"

646 MK/2797 GZ
00:04:36
VOTE REESE 4 PREZ!
FREE ARMOR!
WYATT 4 REP
X MAN 4 PREZ
Jukka
Skronkmonster
HIzKillinIt
Killrkickr
Brooooooce
InvisibleDeath
armor giveaway
my avatar (username = long story)

WYATT

The armor giveaway was kind of a fail. 'Cause titanium armor's crazy expensive, so TONS of people wanted it. But we forgot the only ones who could vote were sixth graders at Culvert Prep.

goldz = MetaWorld money (fake, but still valuable)

So we spent, like, a gazillion MetaWorld goldz buying armor for people who didn't even go to our school. They were from totally random places. Like Finland. Or New Jersey.

CLAUDIA

Reese and his friends also put up campaign posters around school.

REESE/ XANDER/ WYATT CAMPAIGN POSTER

VOTE 2 BRING DA BALLZ BACK!!!
REESE 4 Prez
X-MAN 4 Trez
(tresurer)
WYATT 4 rep

Those were an even bigger fail than the armor giveaway. As slogans go, "BRING DA BALLZ BACK!" is just not good.

REESE

We didn't exactly have the world's greatest posters. But neither did Claudia.

CLAUDIA

This is true. Looking back, it was probably a mistake to let Jens draw my poster.

pronounced "Yens"

I should explain about Jens. He moved here from the Netherlands last summer, he has amazing taste in clothes for a 12-year-old boy, and he is NOT technically my boyfriend.

Netherlands supposedly has tons of windmills (but Jens says there aren't THAT many)

PARVATI GUPTA, second-best friend of Claudia/relationship expert (reads a TON of celebrity gossip sites)

Can I just say, I do NOT get why you won't use the b-word? You've been together for three months! I mean, hello? Put a ring on it!

CLAUDIA

I just personally do not think sixth grade is old enough for boyfriend/girlfriend labels. Although Jens and I ARE going out. Which is sort of the same thing.

And even though we have very different interests, we try to be supportive of each other.

For example, Jens plays soccer on Reese's club team, Manhattan United. (also Xander and Wyatt's team) Whenever they have a game, I ask Jens how it went. And when he tells me, I try VERY hard to understand what he's talking about.

Tbh, this is not easy. Because A) I do not really understand soccer, and B) Jens's English is still a little shaky.

I have also been to one of his games. That might not sound like much, but it was way out on Randall's Island. So to get there, I had to go in Dad's carpool with Reese and his soccer idiot friends. Which was seriously unpleasant.

(Xander farted in car)

RANDALL'S ISLAND = tons of soccer fields (but no subway, so v. hard to get there)

When I told Jens about the election, he was definitely supportive. But also confused.

JENS KUYPERS, close personal friend of Claudia

NOT technically "boyfriend"

In the Netherlands, we do not have the Class President. Or the Government of the Student. So to me, it was very strange.

But I want to be a help. And I am good at art. So I said, "I can make your poster!"

CLAUDIA

It was awesome of Jens to offer to draw

a poster. I REALLY appreciated it. And he's definitely very good at some kinds of art.

But tbh, drawing people is not his strong suit.

JENS

It was big challenge. Because what you wanted was very...how do you say? "Exact"?

CLAUDIA

I asked Jens to make the poster about my new proposal, "Big Siblings." Here's the idea behind it: Culvert Prep is a K-12 school. And I'd noticed that almost all the little kids in first grade are very sweet and nice. But by the time they get to sixth grade, some of them have turned evil.

CARMEN

It's more than some of them. A lot of the boys turn into major idiots—they strut around like they're all that, and they act TOTALLY obnoxious.

And the girls turn into Fembots. Which is even worse.

CLAUDIA

The Fembots are a bunch of sixth grade girls who are completely full of themselves and look down on everybody else for not being rich and/or well-dressed enough.

Athena Cohen's their leader, and she rules them by fear. All the Fembots have to dress and act exactly the way Athena says. This must be very stressful, because it turns even formerly nice people—like my used-to-be best friend, Meredith Timms—into total zombies who can't think for themselves and have to feast on human flesh to survive. I am exaggerating (but only a little)

My thinking was that if we had a "Big Sibling" program at Culvert Prep, older kids who are not evil could serve as mentors to the first graders. Which would hopefully stop them from becoming Fembots and/or whatever you call the boy version of a Fembot. "Boybot"? "Brobot"? "Femboy"??

So I asked Jens to illustrate the Big Sibling idea in his poster. And when he first showed it to me, I didn't really see any problem with it.

THE POSTER JENS DREW FOR ME

VOTE CLAUDIA TAPPER
FOR A BETTER TOMORROW
(unintentional strangling)

JENS

In the beginning, I think, "Okay, not too bad."

But then Toby says to me, "Why does Claudia strangle the little girl?"

And first I say, "Only Toby thinks that. Other people do not see a strangling."

But other people see it, too.

CLAUDIA

Tbh, it DID kind of look like the big sister was strangling the little sister. And I probably should've taken it down. But by then, I had much bigger issues to worry about.

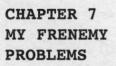

Sophie
Kalisha

CHAPTER 7
MY FRENEMY PROBLEMS

CLAUDIA

Let me just say that Sophie Koh is my one and only best friend of all time.

And I totally have her back. For example, if Sophie had a twin brother who was running against her for class president, THERE'S NO WAY I'D EVER WRITE AN ARTICLE ABOUT IT FOR THE SCHOOL PAPER.

SOPHIE KOH

Okay, that is NOT fair. Because you KNOW being a writer is my dream job. And I'd been trying FOREVER to get Josh Koppelman—who's the editor of the *Culvert Chronicle,* and is TOTALLY ageist, or gradeist, or whatever you call people who discriminate against sixth graders—to publish one of my articles.

not sure if these are real words

And this was the FIRST time he actually put one in the paper! So it was HUGE for me! It was my big break!

Plus, I thought the article made you look good.

CLAUDIA

Whatever, Sophie.

middle school newspaper (actually more of a web page)

The Culvert Chronicle

WEEKLY ROUNDUP

6th Grade Election Is Brother-vs.-Sister Battle

aka MY SUPPOSEDLY BEST FRIEND

by Sophie Koh, special correspondent

This month's sixth grade presidential election will be a real civil war.

Political newcomer Reese Tapper just announced he will run against his sister, three-term president Claudia Tapper, for the top job.

Also running is James Mantolini, who claimed in last September's election that many Culvert Prep teachers are secretly robots.

Mr. Tapper says he is running to overturn the recent ban on rooftop soccer games. "It's so scroncking [sic] unfair!" he told a *Chronicle* correspondent.

not a real word (and spelled wrong)

When asked how she feels about her brother running against her, President Tapper said, "I think it's fine. Everyone should have a voice in our democracy."

But off the record, a source close to the president called the Reese campaign "like, SUCH a total joke."

(Parvati)

CLAUDIA

But Sophie becoming a journalist was only my second-biggest frenemy problem.

Friend + Enemy = "Frenemy"

The biggest one was Kalisha. We're lunch table buddies. And I've always known Kalisha is very, very smart.

But here's what I did NOT know about Kalisha: she's evil and she hates me.

KALISHA HENDRICKS, Frenemy

I don't hate you! We're lunch table buddies!

CLAUDIA

Then why'd you stab me in the back by becoming Reese's campaign manager?!

KALISHA

Extra credit.

CLAUDIA

What?!

KALISHA

Remember that unit we did in social studies about elections? And Mr. McDonald was like, "I'll give extra credit to anybody who does volunteer work on a political campaign"?

CLAUDIA

Yeah...But I thought Mr. McDonald meant a REAL campaign. (i.e. one with adults)

KALISHA

So did Mr. McDonald. But I convinced him Reese's campaign should count. Mostly because it seemed like Reese didn't have a prayer. So it'd be pretty huge if I could turn it around for him.

CLAUDIA

I seriously can't believe you betrayed me just for extra credit in social studies.

KALISHA

It was totally not personal! And I thought it'd be fun. I've been doing a TON of reading about politics lately. And it's fascinating! Like, I used to think it was all about issues. Like taxes, or whatever.

But it's really just a big game. You ever watch cable news? Their political shows are EXACTLY like pro wrestling. Only with old guys wearing suits. And instead of throwing chairs at each other, they yell.

Although sometimes they throw chairs, too. It depends on which channel you're watching.

CABLE NEWS
(artist's re-creation)
(saw this on Channel 44)

CLAUDIA

Wow, Kalisha. That is just totally cynical and wrong. I personally believe politics is NOT about throwing chairs at people. I think it's about trying to make the world a better place.

KALISHA

I know! That's why I thought Reese could beat you.

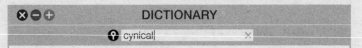

DICTIONARY

cynical

cynical | ˈsin-i-kəl | adjective
1. believing or acting as if all people are fundamentally selfish; 2. doubtful about the value or possibility of something; 3. willing to violate standards of behavior in order to pursue selfish goals

SURPRISED THERE IS NO PIC OF KALISHA NEXT TO THIS DEFINITION IN DICTIONARY

REESE

It was a total accident that Kalisha became my campaign manager. I didn't even know campaigns HAD managers. But she sits behind me in math, and when she heard me and Xander talking about our armor giveaway on MetaWorld, she was like, "Why are you wasting time on outreach to your base?"

And I was like, "Whaaaa?"

KALISHA

So I explained to Reese that kids who play MetaWorld were going to vote for him no matter what. And so were kids he played soccer with.

And in politics, people who'll vote for you no matter what are called your "base."

But at most, Reese's base was maybe 20

kids. And to win the election, he needed more like 49 votes.

So his whole focus should've been kids who DON'T play MetaWorld or soccer.

REESE

I was like, "That is SO smart! So what should I do?"

KALISHA

I said, "Surrender. Because you're totally clueless, and your sister's going to gut you like a fish."

XANDER

I was all, "Yo, don't be talkin' dat smack wit us, K-Town!"

Xander's nickname for Kalisha (I think)

KALISHA

And I said, "Xander, I think the way you talk is offensive, and if you don't stop doing it around me, I will hurt you. Badly."

XANDER

And I was all, "I am very sorry if I offended you, and it will not happen again, Kalisha."

Kalisha is 3 inches taller than Xander (so can def kick his butt)

REESE

I was like, "I can't surrender! I don't even know what that word means!"

(50% chance Reese literally DOES NOT KNOW what "surrender" means)

KALISHA

So I said, "Then your only hope is to make me your campaign manager. And do EVERYTHING I tell you to do...EXACTLY how I tell you to do it."

REESE

And I was like, "Deal."

CLAUDIA

Reese, you realize Kalisha didn't care AT ALL about you, or your campaign, or soccer on the roof, right? She was just using you to get extra credit in social studies!

REESE

Yeah, I was totally fine with that.

CHAPTER 8
THE SECRET PLOT TO DESTROY ME

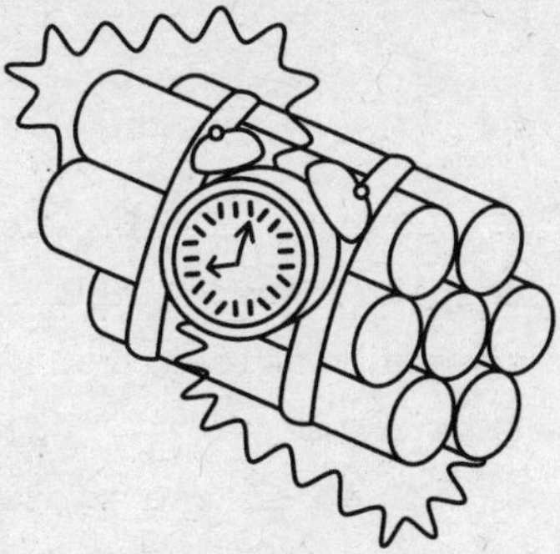

CLAUDIA

At first, I had no clue Kalisha was taking over Reese's campaign. All I knew was that his posters suddenly got MUCH more professional-looking.

Reese's first post-Kalisha campaign poster
(major upgrade over "BRING DA BALLZ BACK!")
(see p. 42)

REESE
A NEW DIRECTION

But I just figured Wyatt's mom was helping them. I had no idea that behind the scenes, Kalisha and Reese were plotting to destroy me.

Most of the plotting happened at a secret meeting after school at the Shake Shack on 86th Street.

SHAKE SHACK: location of secret meeting to plot my destruction (also v. good caramel milkshakes)

SHAKE SHACK

KALISHA

That first meeting was a little annoying. Because I'd agreed to manage the "Reese for President" campaign. Not the "Reese and Xander and Wyatt" campaign.

REESE

The idea was that me and Xander and Wyatt were a team.

KALISHA

I know. But that was a terrible idea. Because your biggest weakness—and as your campaign manager, it was important for me to be brutally honest with you, even if it sounded super-mean—was that people thought of you as a dumb sporto. And running on a slate with two other dumb sportos was NOT helping you.

I prefer the term "soccer idiot" (but same thing)

Also, Xander has no idea how to behave in a restaurant.

XANDER

K-Town was SO uptight, yo! Alls I did was creep two fries up my nose.

KALISHA

They weren't just fries. They were cheese fries.

And there was ketchup on them.

And he put them IN HIS NOSE.

WYATT

I guess if you think about it, that's pretty gross. But Xander does it every time we go to Shake Shack. So I was kinda used to it. And when Kalisha said she was going to quit the whole campaign if he didn't leave, I was like, "What's the big deal?"

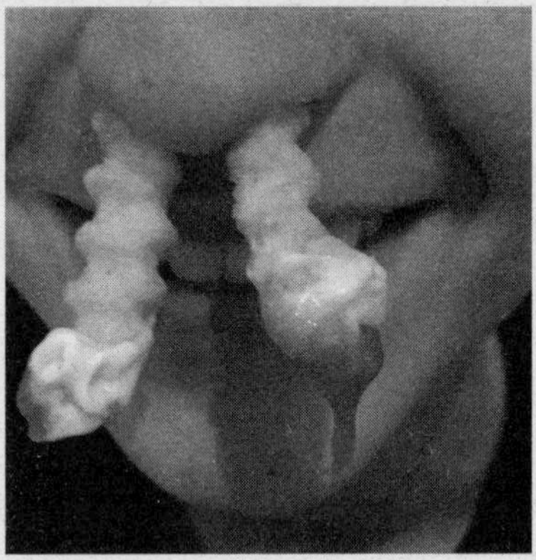

SOOOOO DISGUSTING (photo credit: Reese Tapper) (taken on earlier trip to Shake Shack)

I still think it's uncool she made me leave, too. I hadn't stuck ANYTHING up my nose. So I was like, "Reese! Tell her I have to stay!"

REESE

So I had to be all, "Dudes, sorry. Kalisha's my coach—"

KALISHA

Manager. There's no coach in politics.

REESE

Right. Manager.

So I was like, "Dudes, sorry. Kalisha's the manager of my team."

KALISHA

Ticket.

REESE

Huh?

KALISHA

It's not a team. It's a ticket. Or a slate. Or a party. But not a team. There's no team in politics.

REESE

Right. Okay. Sorry...Where were we?

KALISHA

I kicked out Xander and Wyatt. Then I showed you the polling data.

REESE

Oh, yeah! This part is CRAAAAY.

Kalisha had asked everybody in our grade a gazillion questions. And then she, like, split everybody all up into these tiny little groups.

KALISHA

I used the polling data to split the class into subgroups based on their voting habits. But when I tried to explain it to Reese, he just got confused.

REESE

I seriously did NOT get what she was talking about. I felt like my brain was splooshing out of my ears.

KALISHA

Eventually, I had to draw him a picture.

KALISHA'S PICTURE OF THE ELECTION

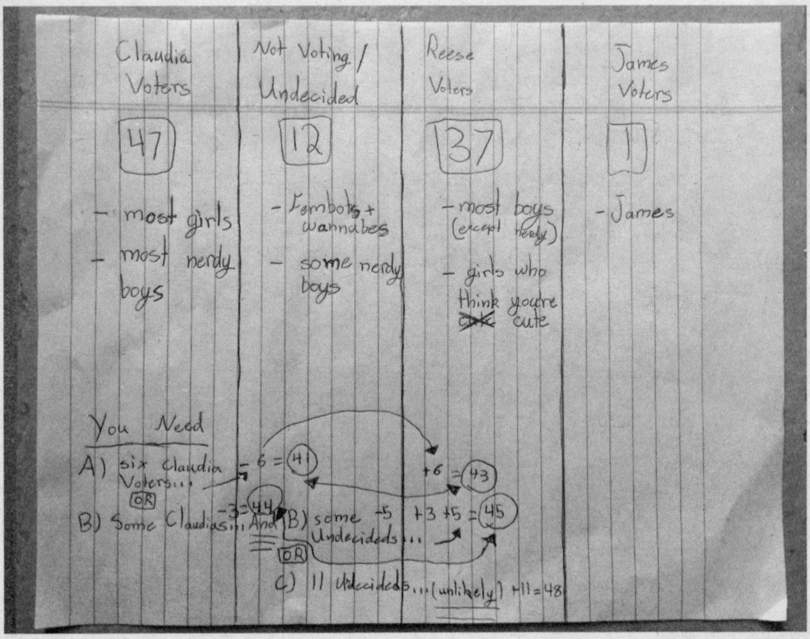

Claudia Voters
Not Voting / Undecided
Reese Voters
James Voters
47
12
37
1
- most girls
- most nerdy boys
- Fembots + Wannabes
- some nerdy boys
- most boys (except nerdy)
- girls who think you're cute
- James
You Need
A) six Claudia Voters...
-6 = 41
+6 = 43
OR
B) Some Claudias... And B) some Undecideds...
-3 = 44
-5
+3 +5 = 45
OR
C) 11 Undecideds... (unlikely) +11 = 48

The bottom line was that Claudia had a solid lead. If Reese was going to win, he needed most of the Undecided voters, some Claudia voters, or a little of both.

So we had to come up with a VERY good reason for people to vote for him.

REESE

Kalisha was like, "Tell me your vision for the sixth grade."

And I was like, "Huh?"

And she was like, "What's the story we're going to tell about WHY you should be president?"

And I was like, "So we can play soccer on the roof!"

And she was like, "We already HAVE the soccer voters! It's not enough! Why else?"

And I was like, "To pwn my sister."

And she was like, "That's not helpful. WHY ELSE should you be president?"

And I was like, "THAT'S IT."

KALISHA

I said, "Dig deep. Outside of soccer on the roof and pwning your sister, is there ANY REASON for ANYBODY to EVER vote for you?"

REESE

And I was like, "No."

KALISHA

So we didn't have a choice. Without any kind of positive message, the only way Reese could win was by going negative.

"going negative" = DESTROYING YOUR OPPONENT (me) with vicious attacks that are NOT EVEN TRUE

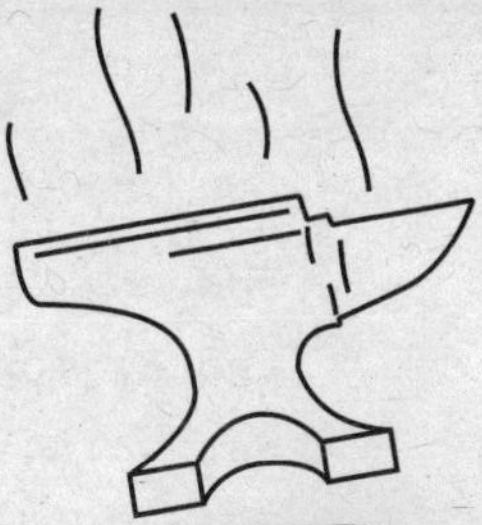

CHAPTER 9
I GET AMBUSHED AT FRIDAY ASSEMBLY

CLAUDIA

The election officially kicked off with candidate speeches at Friday Assembly, which is held in the library at the end of the day.

CARMEN, friend of Claudia/candidate for treasurer

The problem with Friday Assembly is that it's, like, twenty minutes till the weekend starts. So most kids are totally checked out. And it's RIDIC hard to talk to them about anything important. Like global warming.

CLAUDIA

Carmen had decided to run for treasurer because she felt like as a class rep, she wasn't making enough progress to stop global warming. We'd agreed to be running mates. And when she asked me for advice about her speech, I told her to make it A) very short, and B) mostly about how awesome the weekend was going to be. Because it's true that at Friday Assembly, that's where everybody's head is at.

Carmen did not take my advice. And tbh, I think it was a mistake. Kids looked seriously bored even during the scary parts of her PowerPoint.

CARMEN'S POWERPOINT (SLIDE #23 OF 37)

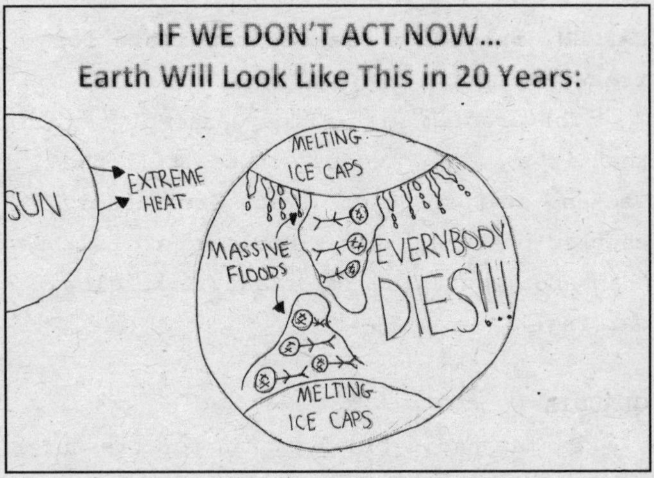
IF WE DON'T ACT NOW...
Earth Will Look Like This in 20 Years:
SUN
EXTREME HEAT
MELTING ICE CAPS
MASSIVE FLOODS
EVERYBODY DIES!!!...
MELTING ICE CAPS

Then Max Esper, who was running for re-election, gave HIS treasurer speech. Like me, this was Max's fourth campaign in a row. So he is basically a pro.

ran vs. me for president in 5th grade (but lost + became treasurer in the next election)

MAX ESPER, sixth grade treasurer/candidate for re-election

This was the complete text of my speech:

"GREAT NEWS, EVERYBODY! There's an 80% chance of snow overnight! Which means AWESOME sledding in Central Park! And last weekend, somebody built a sick ramp on Pilgrim Hill, so check it out! BTW, I'm running for treasurer—VOTE MAX TO THE MAX! Peace out!"

I think it was very effective.

PILGRIM HILL (best sledding in Central Park)

"sick ramp"?

CLAUDIA

It really was. Like I said, Max is a pro.

Then Xander got up and basically embarrassed himself.

XANDER, gigantic idiot/candidate for treasurer

I was all, "WUT UP, six G?? Time ta jump on dat X-Man bandwagon, bruhs! Put yo' X by da X fo' trez and I'ma make dem Benjamins RAIN!"

CLAUDIA

It was just sad. Really.

Then it was time for the presidential candidates. James Mantolini went first. I knew he'd be quick, because after last year's robot speech went on for half an hour, Mrs. Bevan made a rule that James can only give a speech if he stops as soon as she tells him to.

So he has to get the crazy out fast.

JAMES

I started with, "My fellow sixth graders, I have three words for you: FREE RANGE EDUCATION."

REESE

People were like, "Free ra-whaaat?"

JAMES

I said, "Brothers and sisters, we are human animals! With arms and legs that are meant to run and jump and climb! But for eight hours a day, we are IMPRISONED by our desks and chairs!

"THIS IS NOT NATURAL! If our bodies were meant to sit in chairs all day, our butts would be THREE FEET WIDE! And we'd have tiny little stick legs and floppy arms!"

CLAUDIA

As soon as James said "butts," Mrs. Bevan stood up and was like, "Oooookay, James—"

JAMES

"Vote for me and I'll put an end to classroom furniture! No desks! No chairs! And EVERY CLASS will have climbing walls and monkey bars on the ceiling! You want sledding, Max? I'll give you sledding—IN ENGLISH CLASS!"

JAMES'S CAMPAIGN POSTER

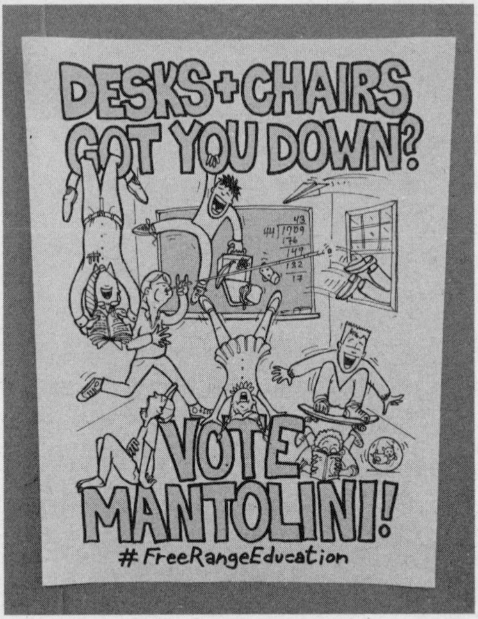
DESKS+CHAIRS GOT YOU DOWN?
VOTE MANTOLINI!
#FreeRangeEducation

CLAUDIA

At that point, Mrs. Bevan grabbed the mic, and James had to sit down.

I was next. I don't remember my exact words, but my outline looked like this:

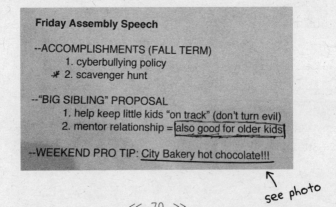

Friday Assembly Speech

--ACCOMPLISHMENTS (FALL TERM)
1. cyberbullying policy
* 2. scavenger hunt

--"BIG SIBLING" PROPOSAL
1. help keep little kids "on track" (don't turn evil)
2. mentor relationship = also good for older kids

--WEEKEND PRO TIP: City Bakery hot chocolate!!!

↑ see photo

Tbh, I thought my speech went over very well.

CITY BAKERY HOT CHOCOLATE: srsly best in NYC

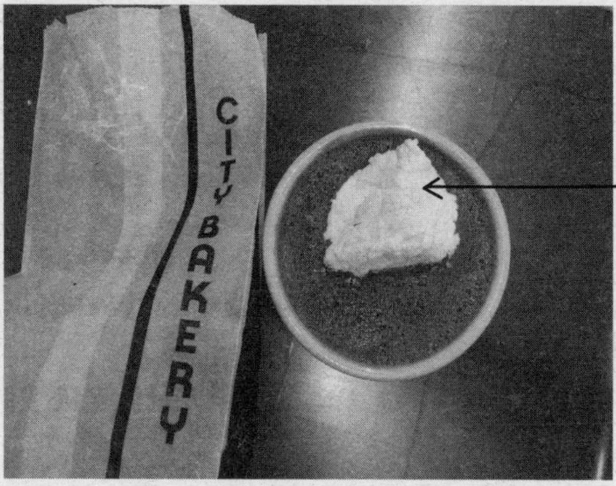
CITY BAKERY

they make their own marshmallows!!!

Then it was Reese's turn. He got up holding his iPad, and at first I thought he was just going to read his speech off of it.

REESE

I was CRAZY nervous. So when I went, "My name is Reese Tapper, and I'm running for president," it came out all quibbly-sounding. ("quivery"?)

Then I was like, "You guys probably know I play soccer. But I don't JUST want to be a soccer president. I want to be a president for EVERYBODY."

CLAUDIA

My campaign slogan in last fall's election had been "A President For Everybody." So when Reese said that, my first thought was, "I can't believe he stole my slogan! That is SO lame!"

REESE

Then I went, "My sister will TELL you she's a president for everybody. But I know the truth. Which is, Claudia has a SECRET EVIL PLAN for when she gets elected. And this is it—IN HER OWN WORDS."

Then I held up my iPad and played part of the recording I'd accidentally made of Claudia.

TRANSCRIPT OF RECORDING PLAYED BY REESE AT FRIDAY ASSEMBLY

...when I'm re-elected? In a LANDSLIDE? I will devote my ENTIRE presidency to WIPING SOCCER OFF THE MAP!

When I'm done, you won't even be able to play it in gym class! You'll get suspended just for talking about it at lunch! I'll get soccer jerseys banned like yoga pants were! And you and every DROOLING IDIOT who ever kicked a soccer ball at Culvert Prep will BEG ME FOR MERCY!

And I will hear your cries.

And I will laugh at them.

REESE

I was watching the crowd while I played it. And everybody's eyes just kept getting bigger and bigger and bigger.

6TH GRADERS LISTENING TO
TOTALLY UNFAIR/ILLEGAL RECORDING OF ME

And when it was over, there was, like, a second of total silence.

Then everybody went nuts.

CLAUDIA

That's when I knew I had a serious crisis on my hands.

CHAPTER 10
I HAVE A SERIOUS CRISIS ON MY HANDS

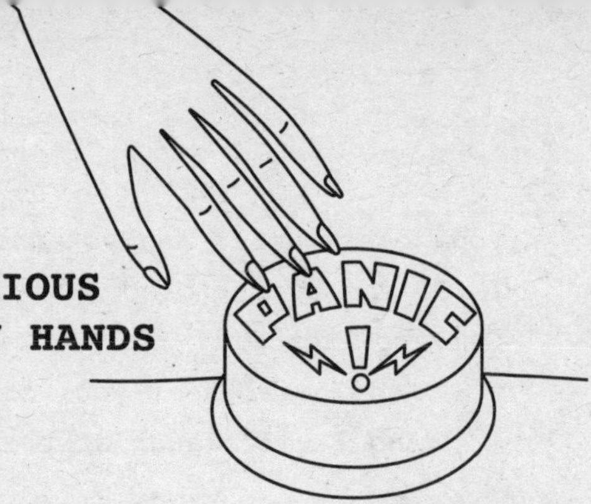
PANIC
!

CLAUDIA

Right after Reese played his totally unfair and probably illegal recording, the final bell rang, and the library turned into a total zoo. EVERYBODY was yelling at me.

not sure (need to check w/ lawyer)

The soccer players were yelling, "You can't ban us! We ban YOU!"

Kids who don't play soccer were yelling, "Are you crazy?"

And James Mantolini was yelling, "Claudia Tapper FOR THE WIN!"

MOB SCENE IN LIBRARY (not actual mob) (but close)

All I could do was yell back, "I WAS KIDDING!" But nobody seemed to believe me.

DIMITRI SHARANSKY, undecided voter

The thing about that recording was, it did NOT sound like you were kidding.

were Claudia voters until Reese played recording

TOBY ZIMMERMAN, undecided voter

You sounded like the bad guy in a superhero movie. Which was awesome!

Except you don't want to go making the bad guy president. 'Cause they're usually psychos.

CLAUDIA

I felt like I was getting attacked by an angry mob. Fortunately, Parvati—who can be seriously fierce when she wants to—made herself my bodyguard, and she and Carmen cleared a path to the hallway.

Then the three of us ran down the back stairs to the girls' bathroom on the first floor, where we hid out until things settled down.

first floor girls' bathroom
(hiding out took place here)

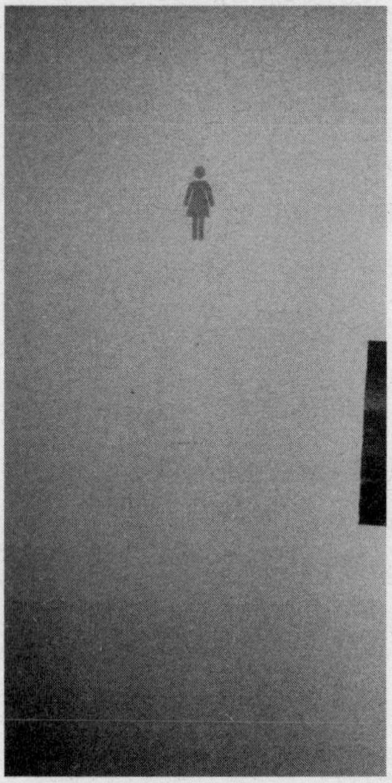

PARVATI

I was like, "Are you okay? Take deep breaths. Also, if you want to cry, grab a stall and let loose. I'll cover you."

CARMEN

I just want to say, I was seriously impressed you didn't cry. Because if that had happened to me, I would've been a puddle.

CLAUDIA

It's not that I didn't WANT to cry. I just felt like it wouldn't be presidential. If you're the president, and there's a crisis, you are NOT supposed to cry.

Plus, I was taking deep breaths. Which actually does help.

Once I calmed down, I texted Sophie.

CLAUDIA AND SOPHIE (Text messages copied from Claudia's phone)

WHERE R U?

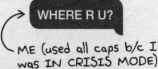

ME (used all caps b/c I was IN CRISIS MODE)

Library. Interviewing people

SOPHIE

PLS TELL ME U R NOT DOING ARTICLE ABOUT THIS FOR SCHOOL PAPER!!!

Don't worry!! Will be v fair to u!!!

CLAUDIA

I was shocked. I'd just been the victim of a totally evil, completely unfair ambush.

And my best friend was writing an article about it for the whole school to read.

PARVATI

I could NOT believe it. I was like, "OMG, Claude, do you need me to go lay some smack down on Sophie? 'Cause I can take her out. She's tiny."

CLAUDIA

I said, "Maybe."

Then I texted Sophie back.

CLAUDIA AND SOPHIE (text messages)

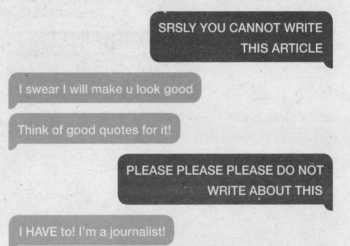

SRSLY YOU CANNOT WRITE THIS ARTICLE

I swear I will make u look good

Think of good quotes for it!

PLEASE PLEASE PLEASE DO NOT WRITE ABOUT THIS

I HAVE to! I'm a journalist!

YOU'VE BEEN A JOURNALIST FOR FIVE MINUTES!!!!!!!!

CARMEN

While you were texting Sophie, Parvati and I went on ClickChat to see if people were talking about the speech. And the first thing we saw was Reese's status update.

CLICKCHAT STATUS UPDATE FOR REESE TAPPER

> skronkmonster Hey, CP 6th Graders—want a leader who ISN'T a power-crazed soccer hater with an evil plan to destroy it? Go to ReeseForPresident and make your voice heard! #StopClaudiasEvilPlan #Freedom #Reese4Prez

CLAUDIA

When Carmen showed me Reese's status update, I knew something was very wrong. Because that was NOT Reese.

PARVATI

We were like, "Hel-lo? 'Skronkmonster' is DEFS your brother's screen name."

CLAUDIA

I said, "But look at that post—the words are all spelled right! And he used a comma!"

So they could see the difference, I scrolled down to show them Reese's second-most recent status update:

CLICKCHAT STATUS UPDATE FOR REESE TAPPER

> skronkmonster So sicked 4 speechz tomorrow I M GONG 2 CRUSH IT HARRRRD!!!!! almost 100% sure he meant "psyched"

CARMEN

Then we were like, "OMG! Somebody's sock-puppeting your brother!"

↖ sock puppet = fake online identity (usually evil)

CLAUDIA

I was freaking out even before I clicked on the "Reese for President" page.

REESE

Kalisha set up my whole campaign page. Plus she pre-wrote my status update. As soon as Friday Assembly ended, she had me post it.

And I couldn't believe it—the "Reese for President" page already had 500 likes! It was SO beast!

KALISHA

There's a site where you can buy likes on ClickChat. It's kind of shady, but it's super-cheap. So I bought 500. It cost me three bucks.

I was going to get 1,000, but there's only 97 kids in the whole grade. So that seemed like overkill.

CLICKCHAT POSTS ON "REESE FOR PRESIDENT" WALL

ReeseForPresident

REESE

503 likes

↙????? (def NOT Reese)

ReeseForPresident Hi! I'm Reese! Unlike SOME people, I want to be a President for EVERYBODY!

ReeseForPresident That's why I'm asking you to help me #StopClaudiasEvilPlan to destroy soccer!

ReeseForPresident It's not just about soccer! It's about #Freedom!

ReeseForPresident Any questions?

ScaredOfClaudia Just how evil is Claudia?

ReeseForPresident EVIL ENOUGH TO #STRANGLEAFIRSTGRADER!

CLAUDIA

→ScaredOfClaudia Ohmygosh! Claudia's totally psycho!!

ReeseForPresident That's why we have to #StopClaudiasEvilPlan!

SOCK PUPPET!!

CLAUDIA

This was terrifying. And not just because the page already had 503 likes. Or because my poster actually DID make me look like I was strangling a first grader.

It was terrifying because I had no idea who was behind it, but they were clearly A) NOT my brother, B) some kind of political genius, and C) totally evil. also D) it was Kalisha (obvs)

I wasn't just up against Reese. I was up against Reese and an evil genius.

I had to fight back. And that meant hiring my own evil genius.

PARVATI

You looked up from that "Reese for President" page, and you were like, "Parvati? CALL YOUR BROTHER."

CHAPTER 11
I HIRE AN EVIL GENIUS

CALLING
EVIL GENIUS

CLAUDIA

Here's what you need to know about Parvati's older brother, Akash: he's the eighth grade class treasurer, he's one of my closest allies on Student Government, and he knows more about politics than any non-adult I've ever met. (except maybe Kalisha)

Also, tbh, he's not really evil.

AKASH GUPTA, 8th grade class treasurer/ evil genius

No, I'm fine with "evil." Evil's good! As long as you put it next to "genius," it's a compliment.

CLAUDIA

We called Akash from the girls' bathroom, and I explained the situation.

AKASH

Tbh, I was expecting the call. Kwame's little sister's in sixth grade, and she came up to us after school and was like, "OMG, MAJOR BLOODBATH at Friday Assembly."

So I figured you'd be in need of my skills.

CLAUDIA

Akash agreed to be my emergency campaign manager. Then he told me to meet him ASAP at the Hot & Crusty on 86th and Lex for a strategy meeting.

HOT & CRUSTY: best-smelling store on the whole Upper East Side

Hot & Crusty
OPEN 24 HRS

AKASH

I hold all my strategy meetings at Hot & Crusty. It smells AMAZING in there. Plus they have these chocolate cigar things that I'm totally addicted to.

CLAUDIA

On the way over, Sophie kept texting me.

SOPHIE AND CLAUDIA (text messages)

Where R U? ← SOPHIE

Need quotes from u for article so u can tell YOUR SIDE of the story

ME → OK but need to think about it

Hurry! I have 5pm deadline! Thx! Luv u!

CLAUDIA

I was still mad at Sophie, but I was starting to think her article would be a good way to tell my side of the story. It seemed ridiculous that people would ACTUALLY BELIEVE I wanted to ban soccer. Or strangle first graders.

So I felt like all I had to do was tell everybody I was just messing with Reese's head, and the whole thing would blow over.

On the way to Hot & Crusty, I wrote what I thought was the perfect response for Sophie's article:

MY APOLOGY
(written on phone)
(never released)
(b/c Carmen and Akash hated it)

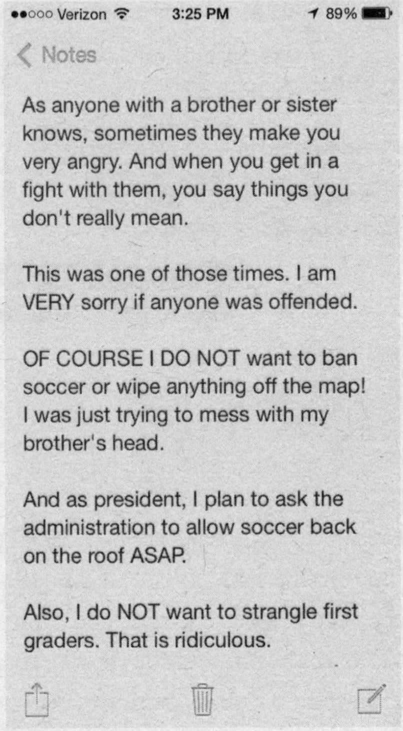
●●○○○ Verizon
3:25 PM
89%
Notes
As anyone with a brother or sister knows, sometimes they make you very angry. And when you get in a fight with them, you say things you don't really mean.
This was one of those times. I am VERY sorry if anyone was offended.
OF COURSE I DO NOT want to ban soccer or wipe anything off the map! I was just trying to mess with my brother's head.
And as president, I plan to ask the administration to allow soccer back on the roof ASAP.
Also, I do NOT want to strangle first graders. That is ridiculous.

I thought it was a very good apology/explanation. But when I showed it to Carmen, she got mad.

CARMEN

I was like, "Hello? You can't put soccer back on the roof! WHAT ABOUT THE SOLAR PANELS?"

CLAUDIA

Then we got to Hot & Crusty, and I showed Akash my apology.

He got even more mad than Carmen.

AKASH

Rule Number One in politics is NEVER APOLOGIZE! It makes you look weak.

And you DEFINITELY couldn't put soccer back on the roof.

Because Rule Number Two is NEVER CHANGE YOUR MIND.

If you do, you're a flip-flopper. That's even worse than weak. It's flip-floppy!

CLAUDIA

I did not understand that. And I felt like I had to give Sophie SOMETHING for the article. But Akash disagreed.

AKASH

I said, "Stonewall her! The media are vultures. Don't give them anything!"

CLAUDIA

I said, "She's not a vulture. She's my friend!"

AKASH

I said, "There are no friends in politics! You want a friend, get a dog!"

CLAUDIA

By then, Sophie was texting me every thirty seconds begging for a quote.

SOPHIE (text messages)

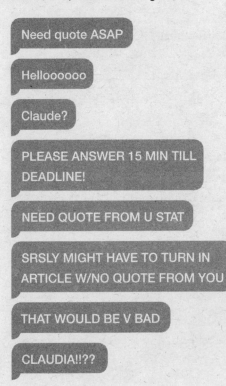

Need quote ASAP

Helloooooo

Claude?

PLEASE ANSWER 15 MIN TILL DEADLINE!

NEED QUOTE FROM U STAT

SRSLY MIGHT HAVE TO TURN IN ARTICLE W/NO QUOTE FROM YOU

THAT WOULD BE V BAD

CLAUDIA!!??

CLAUDIA

It was killing me not to answer Sophie. I kept asking Akash, "Are you SURE?"

AKASH

And I kept saying, "Trust me! Who's the evil genius here?"

CLAUDIA

I would have overruled him, but Akash promised he'd make sure the article never ran in the paper anyway.

AKASH

Josh Koppelman's the editor. And I know where he buried some bodies. So I figured I could get him to kill the piece.

figure of speech
(no actual bodies involved)
(I don't think)
(at least not human bodies)

CLAUDIA

I said, "If I can't apologize, and I can't help put soccer back on the roof, AND I can't talk to the media—HOW are we going to fix this?"

AKASH

I said, "Two words: photo op."

photo op = "photo opportunity" = pic that makes you look good... like this one:
(turn page)

PHOTO OP OF PRESIDENT OBAMA
(feeding hungry people at soup kitchen)

(not technically soup)

It was a no-brainer. You had a boyfriend who played soccer! So all you had to do was go to his next soccer game, take a selfie, and put it on ClickChat with a caption like, "OMG, I just looooove watching my bf play soccer!"

Problem solved.

CLAUDIA

There were so many things wrong with that, I didn't even know where to start. A) Jens was NOT technically my boyfriend, B) it was the middle of January, so I wasn't sure he even HAD a game coming up, and C) the whole idea was just completely tacky and gross.

AKASH

And I was like, "Let me tell YOU some things: A) he's your boyfriend NOW, B) I don't care if you have to fake the whole thing, just GET ME A PHOTO OP, and C) if you don't like it, you can kiss your presidency goodbye!"

Then I finished off my chocolate cigar and went home to start polling the sixth grade so I could figure out how much trouble you were in.

CHOCOLATE CIGAR

EVIL GENIUS BRAIN FOOD

CLAUDIA

I couldn't believe it. I'd hired an evil genius, and his only advice was, "Get a photo op."

AKASH

Give me a break! I had to take a poll first! You can't stop the bleeding until you know where the bullet holes are.

(also figure of speech)
(but kind of disturbing)
(think maybe Akash plays too many violent video games?)

CHAPTER 12
REESE GETS HIS HANDS DIRTY

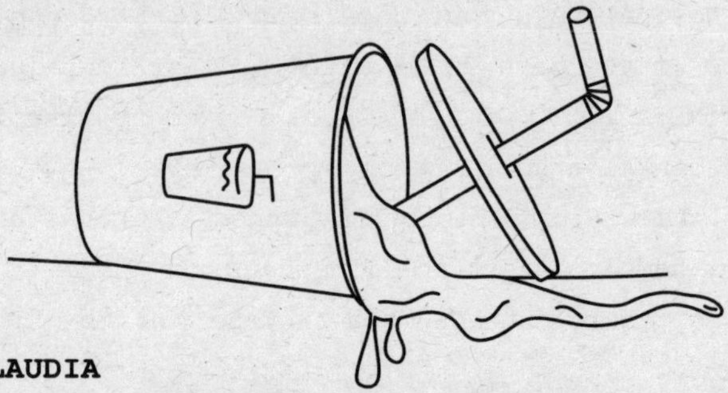

CLAUDIA

While I was meeting Akash at Hot & Crusty, my brother was meeting with Kalisha at Shake Shack. And she was asking him to do something very unpleasant.

REESE

It started in the library after Assembly. All my friends were going, "That was awesome!" and high-fiving me for pwning my sister.

Then Sophie—who I didn't even know was a reporter or whatever—came up and was all, "You don't seriously think Claudia would ban soccer, do you? Like, she doesn't even have the power to do that! Right?"

And I was like, "I guess not."

And Kalisha got ALL kinds of mad at me.

KALISHA

I couldn't believe it! In three words, he blew up our whole campaign strategy!

See, politics is all about telling voters a story. And when I found out Reese had a recording of Claudia ranting like a crazy person about soccer, I decided our story should be, "CLAUDIA'S A MONSTER WITH AN EVIL PLAN, AND SHE HAS TO BE STOPPED."

No offense, Claudia. Don't take it personally.

CLAUDIA

Of course not! Why would I?

SARCASM
KALISHA'S VERSION OF ME
ACTUAL ME

KALISHA

But when Reese admitted Claudia DIDN'T have to be stopped, he killed the whole "#StopClaudiasEvilPlan" story dead. I was going to have to come up with a whole new hashtag!

So I sat Reese down at Shake Shack and explained to him what "message discipline" was.

REESE

It turns out "message discipline" is, like, you decide what you want to say in your campaign. And that's your "message."

And then you never, EVER say ANYTHING except that one thing. And that's the "discipline" part.

And that's what Kalisha told me I was terrible at.

I just felt totally splunked. ← ("sad"? "guilty"? not sure) I was like, "I'm SO sorry!"

Then I bought her a caramel milkshake. 'Cause that's how bad I felt for messing up her game plan.

Shake Shack caramel milkshake (delicious!)

SHAKE SHACK

I was like, "What can I do to fix this?"

And Kalisha was like, "Date a Fembot."

And I was like..."Whaaaa-HUUUH?"

Because I seriously did NOT see that coming.

CLAUDIA

Like I said in Chapter 6, the Fembots are a group of completely stuck-up rich girls led by Athena Cohen. There are four of them: Athena, Ling Chen, Clarissa Parker, and Meredith Timms.

my former best friend (turned to Dark Side in 5th grade)

And there's an even BIGGER group of five or six girls who desperately WANT to be Fembots and will do anything Athena says to get her to like them. Including voting for whoever she tells them to. Or robbing a bank.

I'm just guessing (but prob true)

KALISHA

When I did my polling research, I discovered something weird: NONE of the Fembots vote. Ever.

ATHENA COHEN, Fembot dictator/non-voter

I'm sorry, but nobody who's anybody cares about Student Government. It is just desperately uncool.

STRONGLY DISAGREE (nothing "uncool" about trying to make your world/school a better place)

So's voting.

It's, like, beyond lame. Personally, the only thing I EVER vote on is "Who Wore It Best?" on Red Carpet 24/7.

And even then, I usually vote "neither." Because it is seriously tragic how little fashion sense some Hollywood actresses have. I'm like, "PLEASE tell me you did not pay a stylist to put you in THAT."

KALISHA

The thing is, if you count up all the Fembots and their followers, it's a HUGE chunk of votes. It was more than enough to swing the election.

And here's what ELSE I found out when I did my polling: Clarissa Parker was totally crushing on Reese.

And since the Fembots and their followers are like ten bodies with one brain? I figured if Reese started going out with Clarissa, we could get ALL the Fembots to vote for him.

REESE

Kalisha was all, "Clarissa's totally cute, right? Like, don't you want to go out with her?"

And I was like, "Maaaaaybe. But I don't really know how that works."

'Cause I haven't had a girlfriend since Hannah.

CLAUDIA

Hannah LEFKOWITZ?! Reese, that was back in preschool!

REESE

So it doesn't count?

CLAUDIA

It ABSOLUTELY doesn't count.

Reese on his way to hot date with Hannah Lefkowitz (age 3)

REESE

I dunno. I think it should. I don't remember most of it, but Mom says we were pretty serious. We had playdates and everything.

But either way, dating's changed a LOT since preschool. So I was kinda clueless.

KALISHA

He was incredibly clueless. I said, "Just talk to her!"

REESE

I was like, "No way. Can't do it. Too weird."

KALISHA

I said, "Then text her!" I practically had to write the text for him.

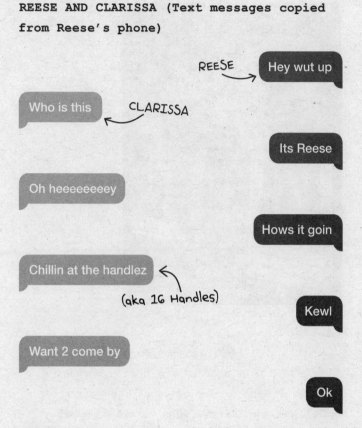

REESE AND CLARISSA (Text messages copied from Reese's phone)

REESE → Hey wut up

Who is this ← CLARISSA

Its Reese

Oh heeeeeeeey

Hows it goin

Chillin at the handlez ← (aka 16 Handles)

Kewl

Want 2 come by

Ok

REESE

I did NOT want to go hang out at 16 Handles with Clarissa and her friends. But Kalisha made me.

16 HANDLES
(yogurt place on 2nd Ave)
(also major Fembot lair)

16 HANDLES
Fro-Yo Hot Cocoa

KALISHA

It was a no-brainer. Hang out with Clarissa for a while, win the election!

So I sent Reese off to 16 Handles. And I was thinking, "Wow—could it really be THIS easy to win the election?"

The answer was, "No." It was not that easy.

REESE

I tried! Seriously. But it was, like...

oh, man. It was NOT good. I think I lasted, like, ten minutes with those girls.

I might've been able to hang in there longer if I bought a yogurt. But I'd spent all my money getting Kalisha that guiltshake. (pretty sure this means "milkshake you buy for someone when you feel guilty")

ATHENA

I'm sorry, but can I just say this?

Reese is furniture. Okay? Like, Clarissa should have invited a CHAIR to hang out with us. The chair would've talked more.

Seriously. It's like Reese only knows how to say one word. And that word is "Uuuuuuhhhhhhhh."

Do NOT ask me why Clarissa was crushing on him. He is, like, SO zero calories.

REESE

I didn't know what to say! All those girls talk about is shoes. And people they hate. And shoes.

But I don't hate anybody! And the only shoes I know anything about are Mercurials. And Clarissa didn't even know what those were.

REESE SHOES FEMBOT SHOES

not much in common
(except both v. pointy on bottom)

So after a while, I pretended to get a text from Mom telling me I had to come home.

And that was pretty much it for my relationship with Clarissa.

KALISHA

It was worth a try.

CHAPTER 13 SOPHIE STEPS ON MY FACE

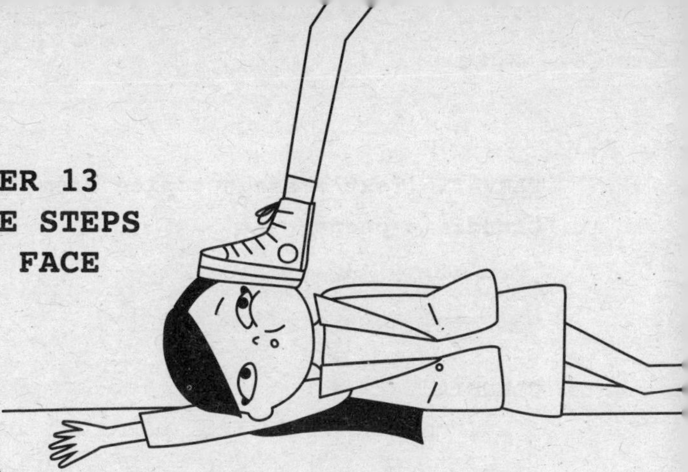

CLAUDIA

I was on my way home from meeting Akash when Sophie texted me.

SOPHIE AND CLAUDIA (text messages)

Had to turn in article w/no quote from you ☹☹☹

That's ok. Sorry I got mad at u!

CLAUDIA

I wasn't really sorry. But I wanted to smooth things over, because Sophie was still my best friend. And I knew she was going to be bummed when Akash got her article killed.

Except he didn't. Five minutes later, I got a text from Parvati.

PARVATI (Text message copied from Claudia's phone)

OMG DID U SEE THE ARTICLE???

CLAUDIA

I checked the school paper's website on my phone. And when I saw the article, my head pretty much exploded all over the back of the M79 bus.

The Culvert Chronicle

BREAKING NEWS: SIXTH GRADERS GONE WILD!

RIDICULOUS HEADLINE (Sophie claims Josh K. wrote it)

Presidential Candidates Vow to Destroy Soccer, Swing From Ceilings If Elected

by Sophie Koh, special correspondent

The campaign for sixth grade class president just got real.

In a Friday Assembly speech that stunned his class, presidential candidate Reese Tapper played an audio recording in which an unidentified girl, believed to be current president Claudia Tapper, calls kids who play soccer "drooling idiots" and vows to "wipe soccer off the map," make playing the sport "illegal," and ban soccer jerseys from Culvert Prep.

pretty sure "analyst" was Sophie

At press time, analysts had not yet verified the voice on the recording as President Tapper's. But many sixth graders were shocked.

"I can't believe Claudia said that," Hunter Arnold told a reporter.

"I don't even play soccer," said classmate Caroline O'Leary. "But that is NOT cool."

no alt. points of view = BAD JOURNALISM

President Tapper could not be reached for comment.

AKASH'S FAULT

However, when asked by a reporter if he believes his sister has the authority to ban soccer if she's re-elected, Mr. Tapper answered, "Umm…I guess not."

Mr. Tapper's campaign manager, Kalisha Hendricks, then broke up the interview and ordered him to leave the room.

this is how I found out who R's evil genius was

Earlier in the assembly, three-time candidate James Mantolini announced a plan to "put an end to classroom furniture," replacing desks and chairs with "climbing walls and monkey bars on the ceiling." However, experts do not believe Mr. Mantolini's plan is realistic.

"expert" prob also Sophie (or Mrs. Bevan)

CLAUDIA

After I picked up the pieces of my brain from the back of the bus, the first thing I did was call Akash to find out why he hadn't gotten the article killed.

The conversation did NOT go well.

BACK OF M79 BUS
pieces of my brain found here, here, and here (ok not really)

JOSH KOPPELMAN, *Culvert Chronicle* editor

There's NO WAY I was going to kill that piece! It was the first interesting thing that had happened at school in months! And it was RACKING up the page views.

AKASH

Josh was totally uncool about the whole situation.

CLAUDIA

I thought you said you knew where he buried some bodies!

AKASH

I did! They just weren't actually bodies. And it turned out he didn't care about them.

CLAUDIA

The second thing I did was call Sophie. And I very calmly asked her to explain why my ABSOLUTELY BEST FRIEND WAS TRYING TO DESTROY ME.

This conversation went even worse than the one with Akash.

SOPHIE

You were NOT being fair to me! I BEGGED you to tell your side of the story! And you wouldn't give me ANYTHING!

And then I STILL tried to help you—like by saying the voice on the tape might not be yours, and getting Reese to admit you couldn't ban soccer, and talking about how Kalisha dragged him out of the room like a boss.

I was, like, bending over backwards for you. And you didn't even appreciate it!

CLAUDIA

It took a lot of time—and almost all my cell phone minutes for the month—but eventually, Sophie and I talked it out.

I agreed to be more available for interviews and stuff. And Sophie agreed to quit stepping on my face.

At least, I THOUGHT that was our agreement. Unfortunately, it did not work out that way.

CHAPTER 14
I (TRY TO) KEEP MOM AND DAD OUT OF IT

PARENTS
KEEP OUT
NOTHING TO
SEE HERE

CLAUDIA

By the time I got home that night, I was seriously spun out. Ashley was there, and she could tell right away I was upset. But I did NOT want to talk about it.

ASHLEY

I was like, "C'mon, Claude! I'm your caregiver! That's what I'm here for! To give care!"

Then I made you a snack. Because you looked like you could really use a toaster pastry.

CLAUDIA

Ashley was being very sweet. And she IS a good listener. At least, during the ten minutes a day when she's not staring at her phone. Which, tbh, I think is a little unhealthy.

ASHLEY AND HER PHONE
(spends 90% of her life like this)

But I was worried if I told Ashley about Reese playing the recording and putting up his ClickChat page full of lies, she'd tell Mom and Dad.

And I did NOT want to get them involved. I'd learned my lesson the first time. see Chapter 5

Even though what my brother had done to me was cruel, unfair, and possibly illegal, I'd decided I was going to either A) handle it myself or B) call the cops and get him arrested. I was definitely NOT going to C) bust him with Mom and Dad.

So before I told Ashley what happened, I made her swear not to tell them.

But then I threw a plate at Reese's head, and she told them anyway.

ASHLEY

I didn't have a choice! It's totally my job to tell your mom whenever one of you tries to kill the other one.

CLAUDIA

For the record, I was NOT trying to kill Reese. And even if I was, I'm a terrible thrower. So the plate didn't even come that close to his head.

I also want to say I am ABSOLUTELY 100% AGAINST VIOLENCE. It does NOT solve anything.

If you can help it, you should always talk through your problems instead of throwing plates at people.

But in this case, I seriously couldn't help it. Because I'd just finished telling Ashley the whole story, and I was totally furious...and then Reese walked in.

And I'd just finished my snack, so the empty plate was right in front of me.

When I think back to that moment, I'm not even sure how the plate wound up flying through the air at Reese's head.

It just sort of happened.

plate I threw at Reese's head
(not actual plate)
(b/c original one broke)

REESE

I didn't do ANYTHING! All I did was walk into the kitchen, and SKWA-BLOOSH!

plate did not actually sound like that when it broke

CLAUDIA

Then Ashley texted Mom:

ASHLEY AND MOM (Text messages copied from Ashley's phone)

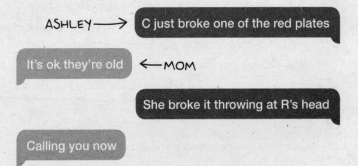

ASHLEY → C just broke one of the red plates

It's ok they're old ← MOM

She broke it throwing at R's head

Calling you now

CLAUDIA

While Ashley was betraying me to Mom, I was in my room texting Dad—NOT to get Reese in trouble, but because I needed legal advice. And he is the only lawyer I know.

CLAUDIA AND DAD (Text messages copied from Claudia's phone)

ME

. If someone secretly records you and then plays recording in public to make you look psycho, can you have them arrested?

What happened, kiddo?

DAD

Nothing. Asking for a friend

Was friend in New York when secret recording happened?

Yes

Then legal. NYS wiretapping law only requires one party consent

🙁🙁🙁

Can we go out for sushi tonight? I had a very bad day

CLAUDIA

Dad did not answer my sushi question. Probably because by then, he was busy reading Sophie's article and/or the "Reese for President" ClickChat page. Both of which Ashley had forwarded to Mom.

MOM AND DAD (text messages)

Read this: http://www.culvertchron...

Also this: http://www.clickchat.c...

OMG THIS IS MADNESS

It's all your fault

What?!

You wanted to let them make their own mistakes

Which ironically WAS A HUGE MISTAKE

Home in 15 min. Will talk to kids then

I am already home

Try not to lose your temper

Too late

REESE

It was SO SKRONKING UNFAIR! All I did was almost get hit by a plate!

And when Mom got home, she yelled at ME instead of YOU!

CLAUDIA

Because you accused me of strangling first graders!

REESE

No, I didn't!

CLAUDIA

Yes, you did! It was on the "Reese for President" page!

REESE

Seriously? That's pretty harsh. I guess I should've read that page.

CLAUDIA

Are you kidding me? YOU DIDN'T EVEN READ YOUR OWN CAMPAIGN PAGE?!

REESE

No! That's why when Mom took my phone away, and then told me to take the page down? I had to get my phone back from her so I could text Kalisha.

AND MOM

REESE AND KALISHA^(Text messages copied from Reese's phone)

REESE →

CAN U DELETE REESE4PREZ PAGE STAT?????

Why?

← KALISHA

MY MOM SEZ I HAVE TO

Tell her it is independent expenditure by an outside group. Supreme Court says they are legal

MOM
(on Reese's phone) →

This is Reese's mother. The Supreme Court ruling does not apply to 12-year-olds. Please delete that entire page ASAP, or I will call YOUR mother

Sorry, Mrs. Tapper! Deleting page now

REESE

I STILL can't believe how that whole thing went down.

If I threw a plate at YOUR head, I'd lose all my electronics for a month!

CLAUDIA

Because you have good aim. So it's much more dangerous.

REESE

IT'S NOT FAIR! MOM AND DAD ALWAYS TAKE YOUR SIDE! YOU NEVER GET IN TROUBLE! EVEN WHEN YOU THROW A PLATE AT MY HEAD! THIS WHOLE FAMILY JUST GANGS UP ON ME! IT'S SO SKRONKING UNFAIR!

← Reese getting way too emotional again

CLAUDIA

Reese, please. We do NOT "gang up" on you.

REESE

Then how come we ALWAYS have to go out for sushi instead of pizza?

CHO CHO SAN: world's best sushi (also not too expensive)
(try the spicy tako hand roll) (warning: tako = octopus)

cho cho san Japanese Restaurant
A

CLAUDIA

You just get outvoted. Mom and Dad and I happen to like sushi better than pizza. Plus, it's healthier.

REESE

SEE??? THIS WHOLE FAMILY'S AGAINST ME!!!

srsly NOT TRUE
(except when picking restaurant on Friday nights)

CHAPTER 15
MY TOTALLY CUTE PHOTO OP

CLAUDIA

My campaign did not hold any public events on Saturday. But behind the scenes, I was very busy staging a photo op to prove I wasn't a soccer hater.

This was tough for a few reasons. For one thing, the whole idea was ridiculous.

And when I asked Dad if I could tag along to Reese's soccer practice at Asphalt Green Saturday morning, my brother shut me down.

ASPHALT GREEN (I took swim classes here) (learned just enough not to drown)

ASPHALT GREEN

REESE

I didn't know why Claudia wanted to come, but I figured it was something sneaky. So I told Dad not to let her. And when he texted Mom at her yoga class, she agreed with me.

DAD AND MOM (text messages)

DAD → C wants to come to R's soccer practice. Do I let her?

No way. She is up to something ← MOM

But what? Can't figure out angle

Probably revenge

Maybe I'll take her, but only if she agrees to get some exercise while we're there?

good luck with that

Exercise offer did not work. Guess she didn't want to go THAT badly

Dad thinks I don't exercise enough (b/c I don't play sports) (but I walk around a lot) (which should count)

CLAUDIA

This was true. I did not actually want a photo op badly enough to exercise for it.

But Jens is on Reese's soccer team, so I thought I might be able to tag along with him instead. That didn't work out, either.

CLAUDIA AND JENS (Text messages copied from Claudia's phone)

Hi! Do u mind if I come to your soccer practice today?

But you hate soccer

I DON'T HATE IT! I think if I watched practice I would like it more

Practice is boring. Only drills. But Ajax plays Groningen tonight - u want come over and watch?

on satelite TV from Netherlands

I can explain you all the clubs

Also rules

Also difference of Champions League vs Eredivisie

g2g

CLAUDIA

Since I couldn't take a selfie at the practice, I had to come up with a whole other photo op. Carmen had a great idea, so I went over to her place, and we used her little brother's soccer ball to take what I thought was a very cute pic.

CLICKCHAT POSTS ON "CLAUDAROO" (AKA CLAUDIA TAPPER) WALL

claudaroo

STOP GLOBAL WARMING!!

(photobombed by Carmen)

23 likes

claudaroo I LOVE SOCCER!

claudaroo And #IDontHaveAnEvilPlan!

claudaroo #VoteClaudia

claudaroo #VoteCarmen

c_2_the_g #VoteClaudia #VoteCarmen #StopGlobalWarming

Parvanana CUTEST PIC EVA!

Kalisha → KaliHendo Seems a little desperate

c_2_the_g Cut it out, Kalisha

CLAUDIA

Like I said, I thought it was cute. But Akash was not happy.

AKASH AND CLAUDIA (Text messages copied from Claudia's phone)

WORST PHOTO OP EVER

It's cute!

CUTE DOESN'T WIN ELECTIONS
(Call me. I have polling data)

CLAUDIA

Akash had spent half his weekend polling the whole sixth grade. And he had some VERY good news.

AKASH

First of all, I have to say Kalisha really did her homework. Everybody I talked to was like, "Kalisha already asked me about this. Twice!"

KALISHA

OF COURSE I did a lot of polling. Running a political campaign without taking polls is like trying to drive a car blindfolded.

AKASH

You must've really gone deep. A couple of kids were like, "Why are you only asking me two questions? Kalisha asked me twenty!"

KALISHA

You can't just ask kids who they're voting for. You've also got to measure intensity. And persuadability. And issue salience. And if you want to do any predictive modeling, you need TONS of demographic data.

Does that make sense?

???? (I read this four times and still HAVE NO IDEA what she's talking about)

AKASH

SO much sense. Hats off to you. I mean, seriously. That is boss.

My name's Akash, by the way.

KALISHA

I'm Kalisha.

AKASH

How come we've never hung out before?

KALISHA

I don't know. 'Cause you're an eighth grader?

AKASH

After this interview, do you want to—

CLAUDIA

AKASH!

AKASH

What?

CLAUDIA

Can we get back to the interview? Please?

AKASH

Right! Sorry. Where were we?

(had to stop interviewing Kalisha and Akash together after this b/c Akash kept getting distracted)

CLAUDIA

The polling? For my campaign? Which you were supposedly running?

AKASH

Oh, yeah. So I polled the whole sixth grade. AND YOU WERE WINNING! You had a small but solid lead among likely voters.

"likely voters" = everybody but Fembots (b/c they don't vote)

Mostly because you got a surprisingly large share of the Nerdy Boy vote. Which was weird. Because in sixth grade, boys usually vote for boys.

So the Nerdy Boys SHOULD have been Reese voters. But in this case, there was one major thing driving them into your camp.

CLAUDIA

The fact that I'd done a great job as president?

AKASH

No. It was that Xander kid. He was your brother's running mate, and he's a total punk. So the Nerdy Boys were like, "NO WAY am I voting for a ticket with HIM on it."

MAX ESPER, treasurer/Nerdy Boy

I don't have a problem with Reese. It's not like we hang out. But he's cool.

Xander Billington, though? LITERALLY the worst person on earth.

MICHAEL KO, Nerdy Boy/likely Claudia voter

I've personally hated Xander ever since first grade, when he stole my inhaler and put it someplace you're NOT supposed to EVER put ANYTHING. Not even your finger.

eeeeeeeew

DYLAN O'LEARY, Nerdy Boy/likely Claudia voter

Xander's SUCH a jerk. Whenever he sees me in the boys' bathroom, he says he's going to give me a swirly.

most likely spot for a Xander swirly (2nd floor boys' bathroom) (Reese took this pic)

I wish he would, because then I could sue him for a million dollars. I'd totally win.

CLAUDIA

When Akash showed me the polling numbers, he was VERY confident. I believe his exact words were, "You are OWNING this election."

AKASH

The numbers didn't lie. As long as Xander was driving all the Nerdy Boys away from Reese, there was no way he could win.

KALISHA

Akash was absolutely right. With Xander as his running mate, your brother was doomed.

BUT...if Xander WASN'T his running mate? And I could find a way to get the Nerdy Boys to switch their votes to Reese?

Then YOU'D be doomed.

↑
i.e., me
(Claudia)
(DOOMED)

CHAPTER 16
THE SECRET REESE-NERD ALLIANCE

AKASH'S SATURDAY POLL NUMBERS
CLAUDIA VOTES 44
REESE VOTES 38
JAMES VOTES 1
UNDECIDED/ NON VOTERS 14

CLAUDIA

After Akash told me the polling numbers, I felt very good about my chances.

This is because I had no idea Kalisha was hatching a secret plan to steal all the Nerdy Boy voters from me.

There are about ten of them in the sixth grade. I'm personally a little uncomfortable with calling them "nerdy," but they seem fine with it.

Nerdy Boys = -smart
-read a lot
-know stuff about computers
-don't play sports

TOBY, Nerdy Boy/undecided voter

Are you kidding? Every 25-year-old billionaire on earth is a big honking nerd. That's why they're billionaires!

So it's pretty much the coolest thing you can be.

CLAUDIA

The Nerdy Boys don't really have a leader. But if they did, it'd be Max Esper.

MAX

I don't want to brag or anything. But I've been coding since I was eight. So, yeah. I'm pretty much the alpha nerd.

AKASH

Oh, please, Max! Call me when you learn how to run Linux. no idea what this means, but Akash begged me to put it in book (Akash = v. competitive about computer skills)

CLAUDIA

So Max is VERY influential with the Nerdy Boys. And if he got behind Reese's candidacy, it could swing a lot of Nerdy Boy votes Reese's way.

But Max and my brother are about as different as two 12-year-old boys can be. So the one thing I ABSOLUTELY NEVER EXPECTED IN A MILLION YEARS was for Max to become Reese's running mate.

That's why the text I got from Sophie on Sunday afternoon was such a shock.

SOPHIE AND CLAUDIA (text messages)

U around? Need quote for new article

About what?

Yr reaction to news that Max is Reese's new running mate

CLAUDIA

I was eating a bagel at the Zabar's lunch counter when I read that. And I was so shocked, I yelped.

And the yelp was so loud that it made the guy sitting next to me spill his soup.

ZABAR'S LUNCH COUNTER
my bagel was here
Don't Be Homesick Gift Crate
I was here
guy eating soup (different guy)

I apologized to the guy. Then I ran outside to call Sophie. But we'd barely started talking when my phone ran out of minutes for the month.

Fortunately, I have unlimited texting.

SOPHIE AND CLAUDIA (text messages)

Why did u hang up?

Ran out of minutes

Please please please don't write this article

I HAVE to it's huge news!

Will use ANY quote u give me. Think of a good one!

No comment

AGAIN? SRSLY?

CLAUDIA

This time, I wasn't saying "no comment" because Akash told me not to talk to the media. I was saying it because the only comment I could think of was, "THIS IS A MAJOR DISASTER AND MY HEAD JUST EXPLODED."

And when you're running for president,

it's very important to act like you're confident and in charge. Even when your head is exploding.

Five minutes later, Sophie posted her article.

The Culvert Chronicle

SIXTH GRADE ELECTION SHOCKER! Longtime Treasurer Max Esper Joins Reese Tapper Ticket

by Sophie Koh, special correspondent

In a major development guaranteed to rock the sixth grade political world, two-term treasurer Max Esper will stand for re-election as the running mate of presidential candidate Reese Tapper.

Mr. Esper is a longtime political insider who has held the treasurer's job since losing his first presidential campaign to Claudia Tapper in early fifth grade.

A political newcomer, Mr. Tapper's presidential bid was considered a long shot until his opening campaign speech, when he played a recording of current president Claudia Tapper insulting soccer players and vowing to ban the sport if she is re-elected.

Despite several requests for an interview, President Tapper has not commented publicly on the recording. CHEAP SHOT

The new Tapper-Esper alliance appeared to come as a surprise to Xander Billington, a soccer player who had previously been Mr. Tapper's running mate.

"Awwwww **** no!" Mr. Billington told a reporter, using a word that is not printable in a school newspaper.

CLAUDIA

The thing I REALLY didn't understand was why Max had agreed to be Reese's running mate.

MAX

It was all part of my plan.

CLAUDIA

What plan?

MAX

My plan to become president.

CLAUDIA

Max, that makes no sense at all! You were running for TREASURER.

MAX

Sure, in THIS election. But I was playing a long game.

I've ALWAYS wanted to be president. But after I ran against you in fifth grade and lost, I figured I could never beat you head-to-head. UNLESS you suffered some humongous defeat that killed your whole career.

And I figured Reese could make that happen. If he beat you, it'd be devastating!

You'd be so humiliated, you'd quit SG and, like, join the math club or something. And even if you DID run again, nobody'd take you seriously.

Plus, I figured Reese would be a total disaster as president. So if he ran for re-election, I'd crush him.

Which meant that by running with Reese in SIXTH grade, what I was really doing was setting myself up to be president in SEVENTH grade.

CLAUDIA

So you were willing to elect someone who'd be a complete disaster—just to help your own career?

MAX

Exactly.

CLAUDIA

Wow, Max. That is just really, really cynical and wrong.

MAX

Oh, get over yourself, Claudia. Sometimes politics isn't pretty.

CLAUDIA

The only person who was more shocked than me when he heard the Max news...was Reese. Because it turned out Kalisha hadn't even told him it was happening.

REESE

She sort of did. After Mom made her take down the "Reese for President" page, I called Kalisha and was like, "I'm SO SORRY I messed up again! What can I do to fix it? Do you want another guiltshake?"

KALISHA

I said, "There's this one thing I need you to do....But if I tell you what it is, you might mess it up. So just tell me it's okay for me to do it myself. And after it's over, I'll tell you what it was."

REESE

I was like, "Deal." Because Kalisha's super-smart. So I trusted her.

But when she called on Sunday afternoon and was like, "Great news! We dumped Xander for Max!" I was SERIOUSLY spun out.

Xander's my bud! We've been friends since pre-K! So I told Kalisha there was no way I could do it.

KALISHA

I said, "It's too late. You already did it. The article's coming out in five minutes."

REESE

I was like, "Oh, this is skronking BAAAAD. How am I going to tell Xander?"

KALISHA

I said, "Don't worry. Sophie was about to call him for a comment. So I think he already knows."

REESE

Then I looked back at the computer screen, and Xander was chopping me into little pieces on MetaWorld.

Which was NOT cool. Because it was a team deathmatch—and we were on the same team! But I guess if I was Xander, I would've been pretty mad, too.

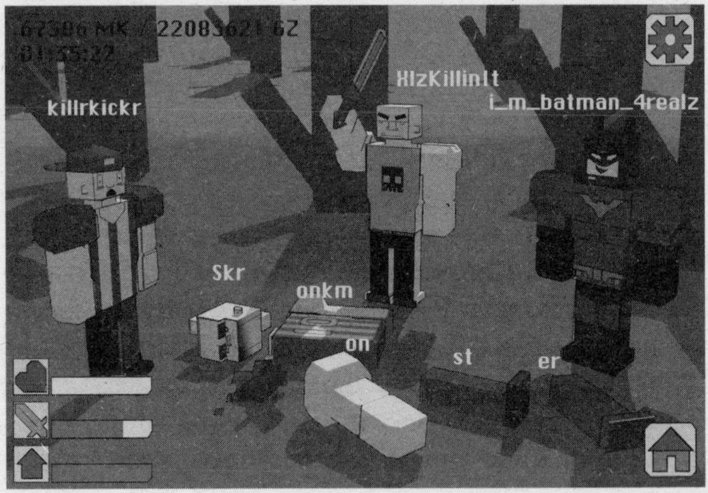
XIzKillinIt
killrkickr
i_m_batman_4realz
Skr
onkm
on
st
er

METAWORLD CHAT LOG

Xander — Reese

XIzKillinIt killed Skronkmonster.

<<XIzKillinIt: DIE DIE DIE!!!!>>

<<Skronkmonster: dude im so sorry!!!!!>>

<<Skronkmonster: it was kelisha!!>>

<<Skronkmonster: I didnt even no abt it>>

<<Skronkmonster: just found out 2 min ago>>

<<XIzKillinIt: TELL HER NO!!!!>>

<<Skronkmonster: I cant shes my coach>>

Wyatt

<<KillrKickr: X y did u cut Reese in pieces? u made us lose dethmatch>>

<<XIzKillinIt: HEZZZ A SKEEEZY JUDAS>>

<<Skronkmonster: kelisha replacd X w Max as my running mate>>
<<KillrKickr: omg!>>
<<XIzKillinIt: DIIIIIEEEEE!!!!!>>
<<Skronkmonster: IM SORRRY!!>>
<<Skronkmonster: X dont b mad! u r like a bro 2 me!!!>>
<<XIzKillinIt: XMAN WILL NEVR FORGIVE U JUDAS>>

James Mantolini

James M.

<<i_m_batman_4realz: yo X-Man I just heard the news. Want 2 join Mantolini campaign? I need treasurer w/ur skillz>>
<<XIzKillinIt: HOLLA DAT!!!!! TALK 2 ME J-MO!!!>>
<<Skronkmonster: thats great!!! u can be James runing mate! so were all good>>
<<XIzKillinIt: U R STIL DEAD 2 ME JUDAS>>

JAMES

It actually worked out very well for me. I'd been looking for a running mate who was desperate and ruthless. So Xander was a very good fit.

XANDER

J-Mo was all, "My campaign's about Free Range Education. You down with that?"

Xander's nickname for James Mantolini

And I was all, "Yo, MY campaign's about REVENGE! You down with THAT?"

And J-Mo was like, "Yeah, that works, too."

REESE

I was SO spun out! Xander totally stopped talking to me. He wouldn't even play on my team in deathmatches anymore!

And Kalisha was like, "Hey—politics ain't beanbag."

I still don't know what she meant by that. But whatever.

CHAPTER 17
THE DEBATE DEBATE

NOT A TYPO

PROS!
CONS!
YELLING!

CLAUDIA

After we got the Max news, Akash and I had another emergency meeting. By the time I got to Hot & Crusty, he was on his second chocolate cigar. And he'd just had what he claimed was a "brilliant idea."

CHOCOLATE CIGAR

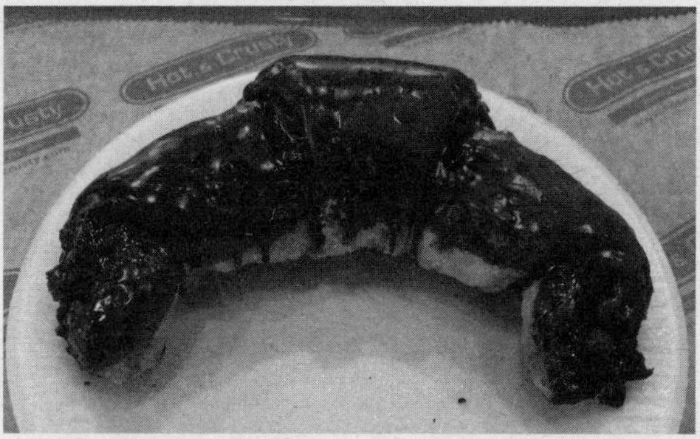

(looks eeeew, but tastes delicious) (Akash ate 2) (then made me pay him back as "campaign expense")

AKASH

All we needed was a debate!

DEBATE = when candidates argue with each other in public (usually looks like this) (ok not really)

Reese's big weakness was that he's totally clueless. Right? So if we had a debate—and he had to stand up in front of everybody and talk about the issues—it'd be a total train wreck! He'd get laughed out of the room!

BOOM! Game over.

CLAUDIA

There was just one problem: there had

never been a sixth grade presidential debate before. Ever. And the election was just five days away.

Plus, I knew there was no way Reese would agree to it.

AKASH

Those were details! You don't hire an evil genius for the details! You hire him for the genius!

Candidate debate! BOOM! If I had a mic, I would've dropped it right there.

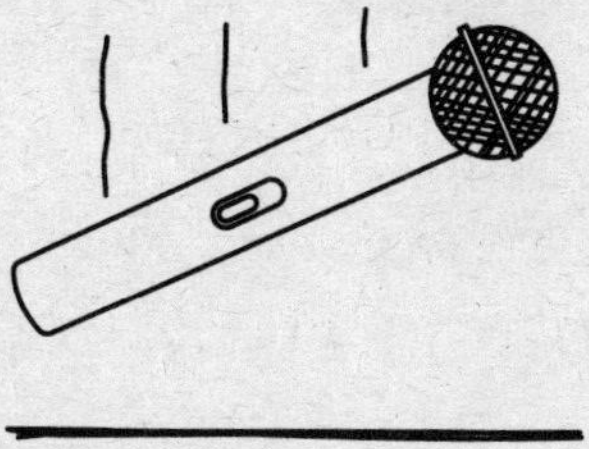

CLAUDIA

So Akash stuck me with the job of figuring out how to make the debate happen. The first thing I had to do was get Reese to agree to show up for it.

Let me just say that I am NOT proud of how I pulled that off. But my presidency was on the line. I absolutely, positively HAD to get Reese to agree to a debate.

And the only way I could do it was by getting Mom and Dad involved.

REESE

IT WAS SO NUTS!!! EVERYBODY GANGED UP ON ME AND I NEVER SHOULD'VE HAD TO DO IT AND MOM AND DAD ALWAYS TAKE YOUR SIDE AND IT WAS TOTALLY UNFAIR!!!

CLAUDIA

but still way too emotional

This was one of those times when Reese was actually right. It's a free country. And tbh, Mom and Dad should NOT have forced him to debate me.

But they did. I don't want to get into details, but it was ugly. And I feel VERY bad about that.

REESE

SO...SKRONKING...WRONG!!!!!!

CLAUDIA

I know! But I totally made it up to you! For like a month afterwards, whenever we went out to eat, I voted for pizza instead of sushi EVEN THOUGH I'd much rather have sushi.

PATSY'S: great pizza (also salads)
(so Mom willing to eat here, too)

Patsy's
Since 1933

REESE

I guess that was cool of you. Making me debate was still totally weak, though.

CLAUDIA

It really was. I am officially sorry for that.

Anyway...Thanks to Mom and Dad, by the time I sat down on Sunday night to write Vice Principal Bevan an email officially proposing a candidate debate, I was able to sign both my name AND Reese's name to it.

I thought it was a very effective email. I listed fourteen reasons why a debate would be good for the sixth grade. And also democracy in general.

I was also very careful not to mention James Mantolini. Because I didn't want to remind Mrs. Bevan that if there was a debate, James might be involved.

I sent the email late Sunday night. When I got up on Monday morning, Mrs. Bevan had already replied:

JOANNA BEVAN, Vice Principal, Culvert Prep Middle School (email)

Re: A Proposal For A Presidential Debate...

From: jbevan@[redacted]

To: claudaroo@gmail.com

Date: 01/25/15 11:37:08 PM EDT

Subject: Re: A Proposal For A Presidential Debate (From Claudia and Reese Tapper)

Hello, Claudia and Reese:

Thank you for taking the time to make your case for holding a sixth grade presidential debate.

I, too, believe that "free speech is the cornerstone of our society."

quotes from my original email

> I am less sure, however, that not holding a debate "risks destroying everything our forefathers fought and died for" and "might plunge our world into a new dark age."
>
> Also, with the election just five days away, there unfortunately isn't time in the academic schedule to host a debate during the school day.
>
> Perhaps we can revisit the idea during the next election in September?
>
> Sincerely,
> Mrs. Bevan

CLAUDIA

This was disappointing.

But I didn't give up. First thing Monday morning, I went to SG's faculty advisor, Mr. McDonald. No offense to Mrs. Bevan, but Mr. McDonald's usually a little more "free speech" than she is.

I only had to mention the first six of my fourteen points before Mr. McDonald agreed to host a debate in his classroom on Wednesday after school. Which was awesome!

Except for the "after school" part.

AKASH

That pretty much un-dropped the mic right there. No sixth grader on earth actually WANTS to watch a debate. If you can't force them to go, they won't show up.

So really, the only reason to do one after school was for the media coverage.

media coverage = article in school paper

CLAUDIA

Akash was right. I desperately needed Sophie to write two articles for the *Chronicle*: one telling people about the debate (so hopefully at least a couple of people would show up), and a second one after the debate telling everybody how stupid I'd made Reese look.

Since Sophie was still my absolutely best friend on earth,
I didn't think this would be a problem.

I was wrong.

CHAPTER 18
MY BEST FRIEND'S MEDIA BIAS IS KILLING ME

The Culvert Chronicle
AWESOME NEWS ABOUT REESE!
BLAH BLAH CLAUDIA

CLAUDIA

Since Sophie’s last article had been totally pro-Reese and even took a cheap shot at me, I felt like she owed me HUGE.

SOPHIE

See, I felt like YOU owed ME. Because both times I asked you for quotes, you wouldn’t give me any! You were totally not helpful AT ALL.

But Kalisha was being SUPER-helpful.

KALISHA

Here's the thing about reporters: they're either your best friend or your worst enemy.

So you REALLY want them to be your best friend. And the way you do that is by giving them stories to write about.

SOOO frustrating
(b/c the reporter ACTUALLY WAS my best friend)

CLAUDIA

This is EXACTLY what I was trying to do when I took Sophie aside before English class and told her about the debate.

SOPHIE

I said, "Great. I'll add it to my next piece."

CLAUDIA

It wasn't until I was sitting in English class that I started wondering what Sophie meant by "my next piece." It must have been mostly done by then, because it posted right before lunch.

The Culvert Chronicle

REESE-ESPER TICKET TO MAKE HISTORY! ←NOT ACTUALLY HISTORIC

Online Campaign Rally In MetaWorld Tonight at 8 p.m. ←NOT REALLY NEWS

by Sophie Koh, special correspondent

In what sources say is a historic, first-of-its-kind event, the Reese Tapper for President campaign will host an online rally tonight on the popular video game platform MetaWorld.

The event, set for 8 p.m. in front of Mr. Tapper's castle on the "Planet Amigo" server, will mark the official introduction of treasurer Max Esper as Reese's running mate.

Excitement about the event is running high among MetaWorld players.

"It's going to be sick!" said sixth grader Wyatt Templeman, who later explained that he meant "sick" in the sense of "awesome," and not its traditional meaning of "unwell" or "barfy."

"This isn't just historic because there's never been a campaign rally in MetaWorld before," said Mr. Tapper's campaign manager, Kalisha Hendricks. "We're also bringing together two completely different types of MetaWorld player."

Mr. Esper, a longtime MetaWorlder, agreed. "That's totally true," he said. "I've practically never even been on a Conquest mode server. So I'm psyched to see what this Planet Amigo's like."

NO ACTUAL NEWS HERE, JUST MAJOR PRO-REESE BIAS

In other election news, on Wednesday there will be a candidate debate somewhere.

totally lame & BAD JOURNALISM to not mention time/place

CLAUDIA

I was so mad at Sophie I almost couldn't breathe. And I did NOT know what to do. Sophie's coverage just seemed COMPLETELY unfair.

I felt like I had to confront her about it. Except I couldn't. Because I was worried if we got in a huge fight, she'd be even MORE unfair. And I REALLY needed her to write a good article about how I crushed Reese in the debate. ← hadn't actually happened yet... but I was VERY confident

But I am NOT good at pretending everything is fine when it isn't. So I basically had to avoid Sophie the whole rest of the day. This was tough, because we eat lunch together.

PARVATI

Can I just say, when you showed up at Ms. Santiago's lunch club for kids who need extra help in math? I practically passed out. I was like, "OMG! I thought you were a math genius!"

And you were like, "Shhhhhh!"

CLAUDIA

Then there was the whole MetaWorld

campaign rally situation. I'll let Kalisha explain that.

KALISHA

All I knew about MetaWorld was that a ton of kids were totally obsessed with it—including BOTH the Nerdy Boys AND all of Reese's soccer friends.

And it turns out there are two completely different ways you can play MetaWorld: "Society" mode and "Conquest" mode.

In Society mode, you build these incredibly complicated planets with their own government and economy and stuff. And you have to figure out how to keep them from falling apart. It actually seems very educational.

In Conquest mode, you just run around and kill each other. It's definitely NOT educational. It's just dumb. And violent.

REESE

I play Conquest mode.

KALISHA

No kidding.

MAX

I play Society mode. All the nerds do. We kind of look at the Conquest mode kids like they're cavemen.

SOCIETY MODE LOOKS LIKE THIS:

Toby

<<TobiusGalacticus: How about a trade agreement?>>
The leader of Planet Toby wants to negotiate a trade pact with you.
Press [a] to lower tariffs and expand trade.

Max's avatar
Toby's avatar
383929393 GZ
00:54:16
EmperorMaximilian
TobiusGalacticus

CONQUEST MODE LOOKS LIKE THIS:

<<Skronkmonster: YA BURNT!!!!!!!>>

68006 MK / 22974333 GZ
00:08:31
Ghostrahm
Skronkmonster

KALISHA

So I thought, "What if we invite all the Nerdy Boys from Society mode to a campaign rally in front of Reese's castle in Conquest mode?"

It seemed like a great way to get the nerds more comfortable with voting for Reese. And since I'd never played MetaWorld, I had to rely on Reese's judgment about whether it was a good idea.

REESE

Kalisha was like, “Think really hard. Is there ANY WAY this could go horribly wrong?”

And I was like, “No.”

But I guess I didn’t think hard enough.

CLAUDIA

One of the many things Reese forgot to tell Kalisha was that his castle was on the “Planet Amigo” Conquest mode server.

And the person who not only created Planet Amigo, but also admins it—meaning he runs the whole planet and has godlike powers to do ANYTHING HE WANTS TO ANYBODY—was Akash. i.e., MY CAMPAIGN MANAGER

So I felt pretty good about the odds of something going horribly wrong at Reese’s rally.

CHAPTER 19
SHOCKING DEVELOPMENTS ON METAWORLD

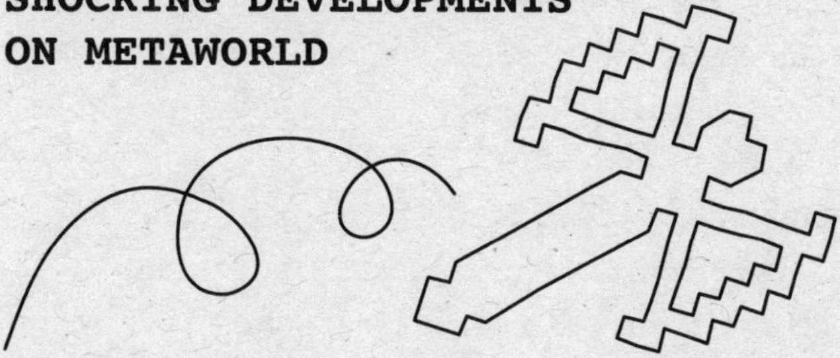

CLAUDIA

When I found out Reese and Max's big campaign rally was happening on a server controlled by my evil genius of a campaign manager, I got very excited.

And then I got very disappointed.

Because when it came to using his admin powers to mess with people, Akash was RIDICULOUSLY non-evil.

AKASH

You can't just go griefing people when you're an admin! It's a position of real responsibility! And I take it very seriously. I'm a fair god.

Not to mention a polite host. Like, I have manners. OK? So if a bunch of nerdy

Society mode kids were going to log on to MY planet for the first time, there was NO WAY I was just going to, like, strike them dead with lightning bolts.

CLAUDIA

You could've done SOMETHING. Like making it rain blood or whatever.

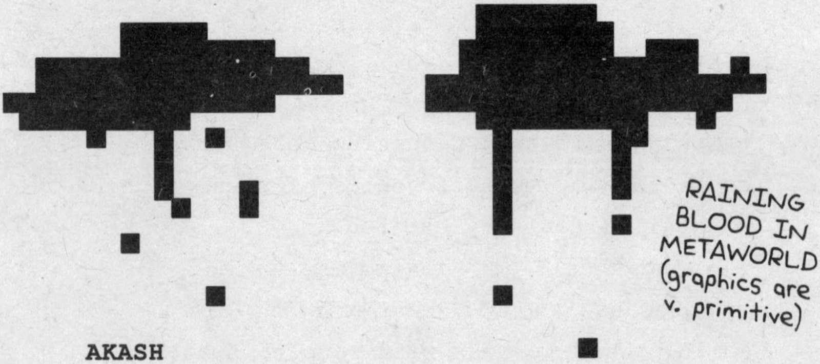
RAINING BLOOD IN METAWORLD (graphics are v. primitive)

AKASH

Do you know how long raining blood would've taken me to code? Plus, I had an English paper due the next day. So I didn't even have time to log on that night.

CLAUDIA

SO frustrating.

Without Akash's help, pretty much all I could do was go to the rally and heckle it in the chat. Which seemed pretty lame.

But I went anyway. So did half our class. The rally somehow turned into the online social event of the week—even kids who'd never played MetaWorld decided to create avatars so they could check it out.

Like Jens.

JENS AND CLAUDIA (text messages)

Hi! Do u know how to make the MetaWorld person?

Why?

I am interested for rally

Call me and I will walk you through it

CLAUDIA

I was pretty surprised Jens wanted to go to the rally. But it seemed like a good chance to hang out together. So I told him how to create an avatar and log on to Planet Amigo. Then he picked me up at my hut before the rally.

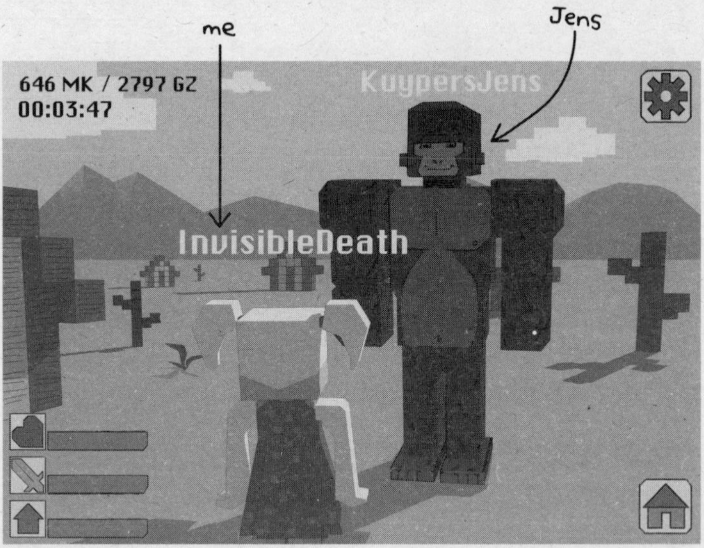
me
Jens
646 MK / 2797 GZ
00:03:47
KuypersJens
InvisibleDeath

<<KuypersJens: Claudia?>>

<<InvisibleDeath: Hi!!>>

<<KuypersJens: Y r u called "Invisible Death?">>

<<InvisibleDeath: Long story. Why r u a gorilla?>>

<<KuypersJens: I like gorillas>>

see my first oral history (The Tapper Twins Go to War) (With Each Other)

CLAUDIA

I wasn't the only person who had a date for the campaign rally. About half an hour before it started, Kalisha showed up at our apartment.

KALISHA

I needed to be sitting next to Reese during the rally. Because this was a VERY important event. So there was no way I was going to let him type his own chat messages.

REESE

It totally wasn't a big deal that Kalisha came over. I don't know why Ashley thought she had to text Mom about it.

ASHLEY AND MOM (text messages)

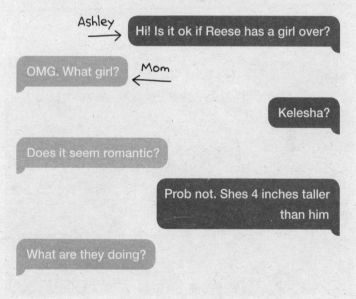

Ashley → Hi! Is it ok if Reese has a girl over?

OMG. What girl? ← Mom

Kelesha?

Does it seem romantic?

Prob not. Shes 4 inches taller than him

What are they doing?

Shes typing on his computer. Think maybe hes paying her 2 do his homework???

If she's good at math, give her my number and ask her to call me to discuss tutoring R

CLAUDIA

When we got close to Reese's castle, I was pretty annoyed to see a huge crowd of avatars in front of it.

But at least the news media wasn't covering the event.

646 MK/2797 GZ
00:05:26
Kuypers
#FREEDOM
VOTE REESE-MAX!
nightsfaker
WeLoveReese
Reese4Freedom ReeseFan

SOPHIE

My parents don't let me use electronics on school nights unless it's for homework. So I couldn't cover the rally in person. Or in avatar. Or whatever you call it.

CLAUDIA

When Jens and I got close, I saw there was a VIP section set up for all the Nerdy Boys coming over from Society mode. Unlike the Conquest mode thugs, the Society moders didn't have weapons. And some of their avatars looked pretty cool.

646 MK/2797 GZ
00:06:02
EmperorMaximilian
Skronkmonster
VOTE REESE
El Presidente
Shabakazam
InvisibleDeath

VIP section

JENS

The guys in VIP were for sure dressed good.

CLAUDIA

Jens and I stood right behind the VIP section, so we had a front-row seat for everything that happened.

And what happened...was pretty crazy.

METAWORLD CHAT LOG

Kalisha typing on Reese's account

<<Skronkmonster: Hi, everybody! Welcome to my castle, and thank you all for coming to this historic event!!!>>
<<Reese4Freedom: YAY!!>>
<<WeLoveReese: WHOOOOOOO!>>
<<nightstaker: MOVE GORRILA cant see past ur big head>>
<<KuypersJens: sorry>>
<<ReeseFan: EXCITING!!!!!!!!!!!>>
<<Skronkmonster: It's SO great to see you here, because that's what this campaign is all about: YOU! I want to be #APresidentForEverybody!>>
<<ReeseFan: PREACH IT!>>
<<WeLoveReese: WE LUV U REESE>>

sock puppets/friends of Kalisha

Hunter A.

<<Reese4Freedom: #FREEDOM>>

Wenzhi <<Wenzamura: Is there free armor>>

<<Skronkmonster: That's why I'm SO EXCITED to join forces with Max Esper! Max and I are VERY different-but we BOTH believe in #Freedom!>>

<<Reese4Freedom: #FREEDOM>>

<<ReeseFan: GO MAX!>>

<<WeLoveReese: #VoteReeseMax!>>

<<Wenzamura: srsly what abt armor I hrd u give it away>>

<<Skronkmonster: Take it away, Max!>>

Max <<EmperorMaximilian: Thank u! Thank u! I just flew in from Planet Esperience, and boy, are my arms tired!>>

????!!!! <<MaxAssassin: DIIIIEEEEEE>>

MaxAssassin killed EmperorMaximilian.

CLAUDIA

I think I speak for everybody when I say it was a huge shock to see a giant avatar in a black mask rush the stage and cut Max in half with an axe.

I was so stunned I didn't even think to take a screenshot until at least five seconds later. By that point, a second masked avatar had joined the first one, and they were slaughtering the whole VIP section.

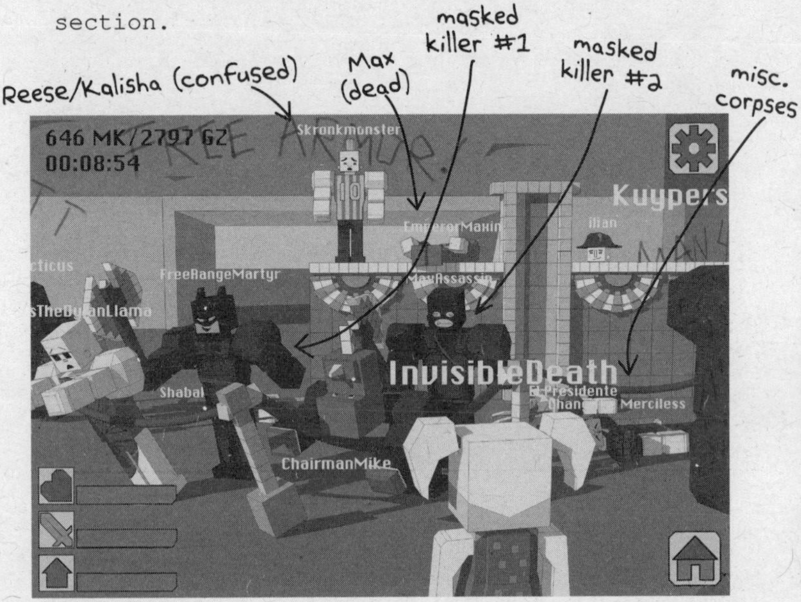
masked killer #1
Max (dead)
masked killer #2
Reese/Kalisha (confused)
misc. corpses
646 MK/2797 GZ
00:08:54
Skronkmonster
Kuypers
FreeRangeMartyr
InvisibleDeath
ElPresidente
Merciless
Shabal
ChairmanMike

Atticus W. (Nerdy Boy)

MaxAssassin killed ElPresidente.

???!!! FreeRangeMartyr killed ChangTheMerciless.

Tucker <<numbah_tehn: OMG THIS IS NUTS>> Dave C. (Nerdy Boy)

<<ReeseFan: Kalisha is this part of rally>>

<<Skronkmonster: NO!>>

<<Wenzamura: this is awesome!>>

CLAUDIA

By then, I could hear Reese and Kalisha yelling at each other in the next room.

REESE

Kalisha was like, "WHAT'S HAPPENING?"

And I was like, "It's an ambush! Get out your sword and kill that guy!"

But she didn't know how to use a sword. And she wouldn't give me the laptop. Which was seriously annoying.

CLAUDIA

Kalisha wasn't the only one who couldn't use a sword. The Society mode nerds were pretty helpless, too.

METAWORLD CHAT LOG

Michael K. (Nerdy Boy)

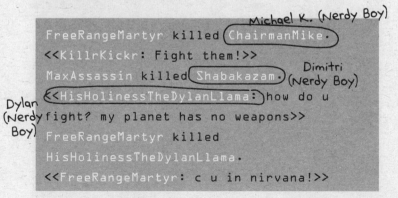

FreeRangeMartyr killed ChairmanMike.

<<KillrKickr: Fight them!>>

Dimitri (Nerdy Boy)

MaxAssassin killed Shabakazam.

Dylan (Nerdy Boy)

<<HisHolinessTheDylanLlama: how do u fight? my planet has no weapons>>

FreeRangeMartyr killed HisHolinessTheDylanLlama.

<<FreeRangeMartyr: c u in nirvana!>>

<<Skronkmonster: EVERYBODY RUN AWAY!!!>>
<<KillrKickr: no fight them!!>>
<<numbah_tehn: BEST RALLY EVER>>
<<TobiusGalacticus: what button is run>>
MaxAssassin killed TobiusGalacticus.
<<TobiusGalacticus: o no my head is cut off>> Toby (Nerdy Boy)
<<KuypersJens: wow this is terible>>
<<InvisibleDeath: I had nothing to do with this>>

REESE

By the time I got the laptop away from Kalisha so I could fight back, all the Society mode dudes were skronked. And the two bad guys had logged off.

dead Society mode nerds
Reese (confused)
killers were here (but logged off)
00:10:21
Skronkmonster
killrkickr
ChongTheMerciless
Chair
HisHolinessTheDylanLlama

CLAUDIA

The MetaWorld Massacre took out every single Nerdy Boy Reese was trying to win over.

And I'd be lying if I said I didn't really, really enjoy all the yelling I heard coming from Reese's room.

KALISHA

I just want to remind everybody I KNEW NOTHING about MetaWorld.

So the massive security failure and all its tragic consequences? Totally Reese's fault.

REESE

No way! You're the one who told me to keep my army in my castle so I wouldn't look like a thug!

And if we'd given everybody armor like I wanted, none of those guys would've died!

Actually, they still would've died. Just, like, not as fast.

CLAUDIA

The situation did NOT look good for Reese's campaign. And Kalisha knew it.

ASHLEY AND MOM (text messages)

Tutoring prob not going 2 work out

Why not?

Lots of yelling from bedroom right now

Not surprised. Doing math w/Reese can be frustrating ☹

CLAUDIA

I have to give Kalisha credit, though: within minutes of the massacre, she was working the media to blame the whole thing on me. And she almost got away with it. “media” = Sophie)

Almost.

CHAPTER 20
THE RUSH TO JUDGMENT

WANTED
FOR METAWORLD MASSACRE

CLAUDIA

To this day, nobody's ever come forward to admit they were the "MaxAssassin" and "FreeRangeMartyr" avatars who killed everybody at the rally.

But it was obviously Xander and James.

JAMES

That's ridiculous! As leader of the Free Range Education movement, I'm against violence in ALL its forms.

But this is the kind of tragedy you get when you force sixth graders to sit at their desks for eight hours a day.

So even though I believe the killers should be brought to justice, I also think we need to address the root causes of this violence.

XANDER

Gotta get with dat Free Range program, y'all! Put yo' X by da X to get rid o' dem desks and chairs!

And peep this, yo: if you gonna be a straight punk and dump the X-Man as yo' running mate? WATCH YO' BACK! 'Cause you gonna get got.

REESE

It was totally Xander and James. I have the screenshots to prove it.

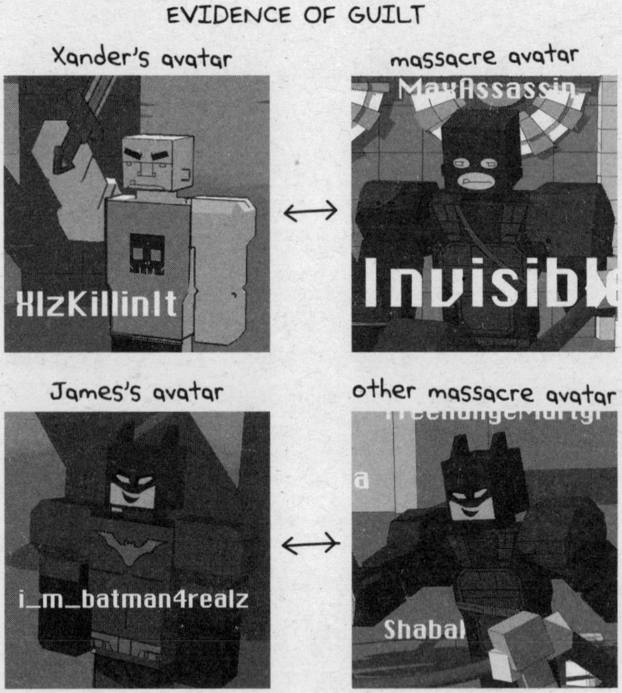

EVIDENCE OF GUILT
Xander's avatar
massacre avatar
XIzKillinIt
James's avatar
other massacre avatar
i_m_batman4realz
Shabal

CLAUDIA

If you knew it was Xander and James, why did your campaign manager blame it all on me?

REESE

Uhhhmmmm...No comment?

KALISHA

All I did was make sure Sophie had the facts. And the facts were that there'd been a terrible tragedy...on a server run by YOUR campaign manager...that just happened to benefit YOUR campaign.

SOPHIE

And to be fair, Claudia—you and Akash DID have a history of killing Reese on that Planet Amigo thing.

again, VERY long story (which you can read about in The Tapper Twins Go to War)

CLAUDIA

When Sophie called for an interview and basically accused me and Akash of planning the whole massacre, I pretty much lost it. EVERYTHING I was mad at her about just came barfing out.

And then everything SHE was mad at ME for came barfing out of HER. even though most of it was v. unfair

SOPHIE

It was pretty ugly. I don't want to get into details—

CLAUDIA

I don't, either.

SOPHIE

But yeah. It was a lot of drama.

It really seemed like it cleared the air, though. Like, I heard where you were coming from. And you heard where I was coming from.

CLAUDIA

When Sophie's report on the massacre showed up in the *Chronicle* the next morning, it still didn't seem completely fair. But at least it wasn't a total hit job on me. And it seemed like Sophie was finally figuring out she couldn't trust Kalisha.

The Culvert Chronicle

MASSACRE IN METAWORLD!

6th grade Treasurer Esper's Avatar, 6 Others Slaughtered At Online Rally

by Sophie Koh, special correspondent

Tragedy struck last night's online rally for the Reese Tapper-Max Esper sixth grade election ticket as masked avatars with battle-axes attacked the avatars of Mr. Esper and half a dozen members of the audience.

Sophie does not play video games (so totally clueless re. MetaWorld)

All seven avatars were reported dead and will have to be replaced if their owners want to keep playing MetaWorld, according to people with knowledge of the situation.

The identities of the two attackers are still unknown. Late last night, a group calling itself The Popular Front For Free Range Education emailed the *Chronicle* to claim credit for the massacre.

However, it is unclear whether this is a real group that actually exists.

Kalisha Hendricks, manager of the Tapper campaign, tried to blame Mr. Tapper's chief rival, current sixth grade president Claudia Tapper, for the online violence.

"This senseless tragedy took place on the 'Planet Amigo' server, which is owned by Claudia's campaign manager," she said, referring to eighth grader Akash Gupta. "Coincidence? I don't think so."

INSANELY CHEAP SHOT

But Mr. Gupta dismissed this claim, stating that he had spent the night writing an English paper. "I haven't even logged on since Friday," he said.

He also explained that Planet Amigo is a "Conquest mode" server on which players compete in "deathmatches."

According to Mr. Gupta, "If you spend more than ten minutes on Planet Amigo, and you DON'T die a horrible death? YOU'RE DOING IT WRONG."

Sources familiar with Planet Amigo confirmed that this is probably true.

It is still unclear what impact the massacre will have on Friday's election. But the issue is sure to be raised during Wednesday's first-ever candidate debate, which will be held after school in room 432 (Mr. McDonald's classroom).

SHOULD HAVE BEEN ITS OWN ARTICLE ☹

CLAUDIA

Even though I had nothing to do with the attack, I was seriously hoping it'd mess up Reese's chances of winning over the Nerdy Boys.

But when Akash polled them, it turned out the massacre actually HELPED Reese.

AKASH

All it did was make the Nerdy Boys realize how much cooler Conquest mode is than Society mode. Like, within 24 hours, they were all hacking each other to pieces in Planet Amigo deathmatches.

DAVE CHANG, Nerdy Boy/MetaWorld player

Conquest mode's SO much more fun! Even when my avatar was getting cut in half at that rally, I was thinking, "This is WAY cooler than Society mode."

And when I started playing deathmatches, Reese gave me this awesome suit of titanium armor! So I decided to vote for him.

AKASH

The polling numbers were bleak. After the MetaWorld rally, we lost all but one of the Nerdy Boys. Which put Reese in the lead by exactly three votes.

CLAUDIA

By then, it was Tuesday night. And the election was scheduled for Friday. So if I was going to turn things around, it pretty much HAD to be at Wednesday's debate.

KALISHA

It's true. At that point, the debate was your only hope.

That's why I told Reese not to show up for it.

CHAPTER 21
DEBATE PREP: MY ONLY HOPE

AKASH'S TUESDAY NIGHT POLL NUMBERS
CLAUDIA VOTES 41
REESE VOTES 44
JAMES VOTES 2
UNDECIDED/ NON VOTERS 10

REESE

I just want to say, even though it was TOTALLY UNFAIR that Mom and Dad made me agree to the debate? There was NEVER any chance I wasn't going to show up. Because I gave my word. And word is bond.

↑ pretty sure Reese stole that phrase from Xander

CLAUDIA

Oh, really? So when you faked a cough at breakfast that morning, it was a total coincidence?

REESE

It wasn't fake! I really DID have something weird in my throat that made me think I wouldn't be able to talk for a couple of days.

CLAUDIA

And that text from Dad had nothing to do

with the weird thing in your throat suddenly disappearing?

REESE

No! I saw that text and was like, "I have NO CLUE what Dad's talking about."

DAD AND REESE (Text messages copied from Dad's phone)

Hey, buddy—just a reminder that if you don't debate your sister like you promised, you will lose phone for a month

What if Im sick

Then Ashley will take you to Dr. Rosenfeld. And if you're not really sick, you will lose phone for TWO months

Its ok feeling better now

CLAUDIA

My biggest pre-debate challenge—aside from making sure Reese actually showed up—was making sure an audience would show up, too.

And Kalisha did not exactly make this easy.

KALISHA

Reese was ahead in the polls. So there was no upside to having a debate. All it could do was hurt us.

But if he absolutely HAD to show up, the fewer people that saw it, the better.

CLAUDIA

I get that, Kalisha. I do. But I personally do NOT think it was ethical for you to change all my signs.

KALISHA

You can't prove that was me.

MY ORIGINAL DEBATE POSTER...

DEBATE TODAY!!!
3:00 PM
ROOM 432
BE THERE!!!

...AND KALISHA'S EDITS
(can't prove she did it)
(but she did)

DEBATE TOMORROW
3:00 PM
ROOM 310
ADMISSION $20!!!

CLAUDIA

And spreading those rumors on ClickChat was a TOTAL cheap shot.

CLICKCHAT POSTS ON "CLAUDAROO" (AKA CLAUDIA TAPPER) WALL

claudaroo

claudaroo HEY, EVERYBODY—COME TO THE BIG DEBATE TODAY AFTER SCHOOL IN MR. MCDONALD'S CLASSROOM! It'll be fun!

KaliHendo If you go, wear a head scarf. Lice problem still very serious in Mr. McDonald's room

claudaroo There's no lice problem in Mr. McDonald's room!

KaliHendo Trying to keep it quiet so kids don't panic? Gotcha. NO LICE PROBLEM IN MR. MCDONALD'S ROOM, PEOPLE

claudaroo THERE IS NO LICE PROBLEM, KALISHA!!!

KaliHendo #LiceProblem

KALISHA

I'm not saying I'm proud of it. But if you were me, and you'd seen the debate prep we tried to do with Reese at lunch that day? You would've been desperate, too.

REESE

Kalisha and Max were like, "What's your position on cyberbullying?" And I was like, "What's that mean?"

And they were like, "You don't know what cyberbullying is?"

And I was like, "No...I don't know what a position is."

KALISHA

It was scary. Lunch is only half an hour long. So it would have taken a MONTH of lunches to make Reese non-clueless.

REESE

Kalisha told me since I didn't know anything about the issues, no matter what the question was, I should just say, "Freedom."

KALISHA

It made sense. If it was a question

about soccer on the roof, he'd say, "Kids should have the freedom to do that."

If it was cyberbullying, "Kids should have the freedom to write what they want online."

If it was about Spirit Week, "Kids should have the freedom to wear boxer shorts on Pajama Day."

MAX

Then I pointed out that Reese had two minutes for each question. And he couldn't fill two whole minutes just saying "freedom."

REESE

So Kalisha told me to start every answer by saying what a great question it was, and how important it was for the future of Culvert Prep. And THEN I should say "freedom."

I was like, "I don't think this is going to go so good."

And Kalisha was like, "Don't worry. If it looks bad, I'll pull the fire alarm."

pulling alarm w/no fire = INSANELY BAD and ILLEGAL (also unethical)

4-4
FIRE ALARM

CLAUDIA

While Kalisha was trying to make my brother non-clueless, I was on the other side of the cafeteria, having a very important conversation with Sophie.

Because Mr. McDonald had decided that as the sixth grade's only member of the media, Sophie should be the debate moderator.

moderator = person who asks all the questions

SOPHIE

You showed me Akash's polling numbers. Which were kind of shocking—like, up until then, I didn't actually think there was any chance Reese could beat you. So finding out you were losing was a real "OMG" moment.

But as a journalist—AND a debate moderator—I had to be fair and impartial to all the candidates.

So when you started telling me what questions to ask, it was offensive.

CLAUDIA

I didn't do that! All I did was point out all the things—like Spirit Week, the bake sale, the food drive—that you have to deal with when you're president. And that my brother was totally clueless about.

Which I thought was important for voters to know.

I was also pointing out that this was MY LAST CHANCE. If the debate didn't change anybody's vote, I was going to lose to my brother...who barely knows what a bake sale IS, much less how to run one.

SOPHIE

And all I could say was, "I will ask questions that a good candidate can totally crush. So there's nothing for you to worry about."

actually LOTS OF THINGS for me to worry about

CHAPTER 22
SHOWDOWN IN ROOM 432

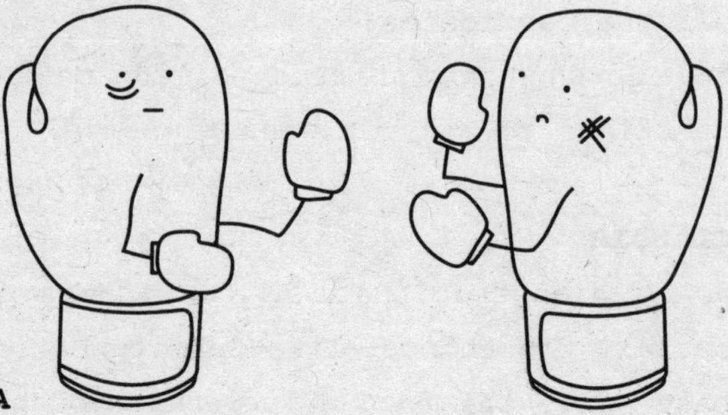

CLAUDIA

Just looking at the audience that showed up for the debate made me realize Sophie's media coverage was going to be VERY important.

Because pretty much nobody was there.

ROOM 432 (with all the undecided voters who showed up)
(i.e., NOBODY)

There were a total of fourteen people in the room, which sounds like a lot. But it wasn't. Because three of us were IN the debate (me, Reese, and James), four were my supporters (Akash, Parvati, Carmen, and Jens), three were Reese's supporters (Kalisha, Max, and Wyatt), one was James's supporter (Xander), one was the moderator (Sophie), and one was Mr. McDonald.

So technically, the only audience member was Bryce Thompson.

And Bryce was only there because he had detention. Bryce is a soccer idiot (so was def. voting for Reese)

BRYCE THOMPSON, member of debate audience

Mr. McDonald made me stay after school for playing Exploding Cows on my phone during class. So it's not like I meant to watch the debate. I was just sitting there.

It turned out to be pretty hilarious, though.

CLAUDIA

I personally did NOT find the debate hilarious. In fact, I thought it was a very sad day for democracy.

Sophie recorded the whole thing on her iPod, and here is the transcript of it:

TRANSCRIPT OF SIXTH GRADE PRESIDENTIAL DEBATE

MR. MCDONALD: *Okay! Thanks for coming, everybody. The format is as follows: the moderator asks a question, then each candidate has up to two minutes to answer. I'll keep time. And please don't interrupt each other. Okay? Great. Take it away, Sophie.*

SOPHIE KOH: *Welcome, candidates, and thank you, Mr. McDonald, for hosting this debate. I'm here on behalf of the* Culvert Chronicle *as its sixth grade correspondent. And I just want to say these questions were prepared by me alone, with help from concerned voters, and were NOT shared with any candidates beforehand. I am being completely fair and impartial.*

XANDER BILLINGTON: *(unintelligible)*

weird cough that sounded like "KHA-BOGUS!"

MR. MCDONALD: *Cut it out, Xander.*

SOPHIE KOH: *The order of responses was chosen randomly. For the first question, it'll be Reese, then James, then Claudia.*

After that, we'll rotate. Okay? So. Question Number One: what do you think is the biggest problem facing the sixth grade, and as president, what would you do about it? Reese Tapper.

REESE TAPPER: *What?*

SOPHIE KOH: *You're first.*

REESE TAPPER: *Oh. Okay. Uhhh...What's the question again?*

SOPHIE KOH: *"What do you think is the biggest problem facing the sixth grade, and as president, what would you do about it?"*

REESE TAPPER: *Yeah. Okay. So. Like...*

[LONG SILENCE]

KALISHA HENDRICKS: *(unintelligible)*

MR. MCDONALD: *No coaching, Kalisha.*

KALISHA HENDRICKS: *I wasn't coaching him! I was just saying it's a VERY...GOOD... QUESTION.*

REESE TAPPER: *Totally! Super-good question. Really good. Like...yeah. Problems are huge. And really important. Super-important. In the future. Culvert Prep's the future! For futuring. It's really...there's, like, future problems. So...*

KALISHA HENDRICKS: (unintelligible)

weird cough that sounded like "KHA-FREEDOM"

REESE TAPPER: *Freedom! THAT'S the big problem. The WHOLE PROBLEM is freedom—*

KALISHA HENDRICKS: *NOT the problem!*

MR. MCDONALD: *Kalisha—*

REESE TAPPER: *I mean, not the problem—freedom's good. Super-good! And we have to, like...it's important to be free. We should have freedom. To, like, play soccer on the roof. And other stuff. Because freedom. Totally. Can I be done now?*

KALISHA HENDRICKS: *YES!*

MR. MCDONALD: *That's fine, Reese.*

AKASH

I have to say, your brother really exceeded expectations. I mean, I would've been happy with just normal amounts of stupid. But he took it to a WHOLE other level. By the time he sat down, I was thinking, "Ten more minutes of this, and the election's over."

CLAUDIA

I agree. Especially because I could have CRUSHED that question. I had a great answer ready. It was all about my "Big Siblings" proposal. And if I'd been able to give it, it would've been TOTALLY OBVIOUS I was the only good choice for president.

But James went next. And he took the whole debate on an express train to Crazy Town:

TRANSCRIPT OF SIXTH GRADE PRESIDENTIAL DEBATE

SOPHIE KOH: *Okay...Next is James Mantolini.*

XANDER BILLINGTON: *WHOOO! YOU DA MAN, J-MO!*

JAMES MANTOLINI: *Thank you!*

XANDER BILLINGTON: *WHOOOOOOO! TESTIFY!*

MR. MCDONALD: *Xander, please.*

JAMES MANTOLINI: *Thank you! Ladies and gentlemen, members of the media, my esteemed opponents...I submit to you that the biggest problem we face today is SO HUGE we can't even see it. We are surrounded by an evil SO COMPLETE we don't even know it's there!*

XANDER: *PREACH IT, J-MO!*

JAMES MANTOLINI: *I'm talking about furniture. Our teachers will tell you they're just harmless "desks" and "chairs." But let's call them what they are: CAGES! Little wooden prisons designed to drain the life force from our animal natures! And* *we've been trapped inside them so long, we don't even know who we are anymore! But today, I've brought along a little friend who I think can help us see the light.*

CLAUDIA

At this point, James bent over, unzipped a duffel bag that was on the floor next to him, and pulled out a metal cage.

With a squirrel in it.

I have no idea how James managed to catch the squirrel. Or keep it quiet while it was in the duffel bag. But as soon as he picked up the cage and put it on the desk, the squirrel started going nuts.

So did Mr. McDonald.

artist's re-creation
of squirrel (going nuts) +
Mr. McDonald (also going nuts)

TRANSCRIPT OF SIXTH GRADE PRESIDENTIAL DEBATE

JAMES: *Say hello to Nutty—*

[METAL RATTLING NOISES]

probably Parvati

UNIDENTIFIED GIRL: *EEEEEEEEEEEK!*

UNIDENTIFIED BOY: *WHOA!*

Wyatt? Bryce? (not sure which)

MR. MCDONALD: *JAMES, WHAT ON EARTH—*

JAMES: *Nutty was born free! To scamper about—*

MR. MCDONALD: *THIS IS NOT APPROPRIATE—*

CLAUDIA

Right here is when Mr. McDonald marched up to the desk and tried to pick up the squirrel cage.

Except he picked it up by the wrong part of the cage.

TRANSCRIPT OF SIXTH GRADE PRESIDENTIAL DEBATE

JAMES: *—on his little squirrel legs—*

MR. MCDONALD: *YOU NEED TO TAKE THIS SQUIRREL—*

JAMES: *That's not a handle—!*

MR. MCDONALD: [EXPLETIVE DELETED]

[RANDOM SHOUTING, SCREAMING, FURNITURE MOVING]

CLAUDIA

What Mr. McDonald thought was a handle turned out to be the quick release lever on the cage door. So when he yanked on it, the side wall of the cage popped up, and Nutty the Squirrel jumped out.

NUTTY THE SQUIRREL
(not actually him)
(but he looked just like this)
(except much more angry)

Then Nutty started zooming around the room, looking for an exit. Or possibly revenge. I'm not sure which.

And Parvati ran screaming for the door.

PARVATI

Excuse me, but I don't know why EVERYBODY didn't run screaming for the door. Squirrels carry diseases!

CLAUDIA

When Parvati flung open the door, Nutty ran out and disappeared down the south stairs.

And that was the end of the debate. Because we had to spend the rest of the afternoon helping Mr. McDonald search the building for Nutty.

JENS

It was very strange. In Netherlands, debates are much longer in time. And nobody brings the animal.

KALISHA

Even without the squirrel, it wouldn't have gone on that long. Because if Reese had started answering the second question the same way he answered the first one, I would've pulled the fire alarm.

Although I have to say, I think the audience really enjoyed it.

BRYCE

Best. Detention. EVER!

CLAUDIA sarcasm :(

Oh, sure. Except for the part where it Killed. My. Campaign.

CHAPTER 23
NUTTY'S NUCLEAR FALLOUT

CLAUDIA

James's bringing a live squirrel to the debate wound up having a TON of major repercussions.

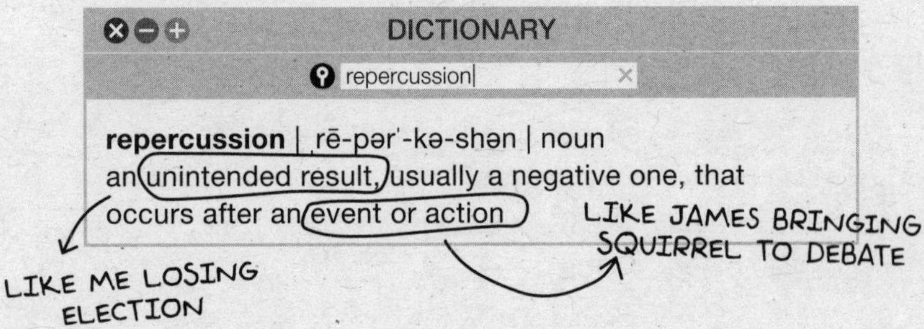
DICTIONARY
repercussion
repercussion | ˌrē-pər'-kə-shən | noun
an unintended result, usually a negative one, that occurs after an event or action
LIKE JAMES BRINGING SQUIRREL TO DEBATE
LIKE ME LOSING ELECTION

First of all, James was suspended from school. It was originally three days, but it got reduced to one after his parents went to Mrs. Bevan and argued that Culvert Prep's code of conduct doesn't say anything about bringing wildlife to school.

They also claimed it was Mr. McDonald's fault for opening the cage. Which, tbh, was kind of true.

Not only did James get suspended, but Mrs. Bevan took him off the ballot and banned him from ever running for office again.

JAMES

I wasn't surprised. True revolutionaries are ALWAYS violently suppressed by the ruling class.

CLAUDIA

I don't know, James. I personally believe there's a fine line between a revolutionary and a crazy person. And you might be on the crazy side of it.

JAMES

I don't expect to be understood in my lifetime, Claudia.

CLAUDIA

The second major thing was that school was closed all day Thursday, because that's how long it took for the custodians to catch Nutty and return him to the wild. Or at least Central Park.

Nutty, post-debate (prob not really him) (but I took pic in Central Park) (so it MIGHT be him)

Coincidentally, a big snowstorm dumped twelve inches on New York City Wednesday night. So OFFICIALLY, Culvert Prep was closed for a Snow Day.

But everybody knew it was actually a Squirrel Day.

The third major thing was that on Wednesday night, Sophie's article about the debate went up on the *Chronicle* site.

The Culvert Chronicle

SIXTH GRADERS GO NUTS!

Mantolini Releases Live Squirrel During Candidate Debate

by Sophie Koh, special correspondent

This afternoon's sixth grade presidential debate ended in chaos when a wild squirrel, brought in by candidate James Mantolini, escaped from its cage and rampaged through Room 432 before disappearing down a fourth-floor hallway.

As of 8:30pm, the squirrel was still at large inside Culvert Prep. Custodians are trying to capture the animal so it can be returned to Central Park, where it is believed to have lived before entering politics.

The episode began when Mr. Mantolini, while making a point about classroom furniture, removed the caged squirrel from a duffel bag and put it on a desk.

The debate's faculty sponsor, Mr. McDonald, then tried to pick up the cage and accidentally opened it, resulting in the escape.

At press time, Mr. McDonald could not be reached for comment.

Afterwards, Mr. Mantolini was held for questioning in Vice Principal Bevan's office. Following his release, he informed the *Chronicle* that his name was being removed from the presidential ballot.

"It's obvious I'm being censored because the administration can't handle my political views," said Mr. Mantolini.

Sources familiar with the Vice Principal's thinking believe this is untrue, and that Mr. Mantolini is only being censored to stop him from releasing wild animals at political events.

pretty sure Sophie was her own source for this

Voting in the sixth grade presidential election will take place during Friday Assembly.

CLAUDIA

Since my whole strategy for winning the election was based on getting great media coverage and making Reese look totally incompetent, this was a complete disaster for me. As soon as I read the article, I messaged Akash on ClickChat:

CLAUDIA AND AKASH (ClickChat Direct Messenger)

Did you see the article?

Brutal. Didn't even mention yr name

B/C I DIDN'T EVEN GET TO ANSWER A QUESTION!!! What can we do?

Gotta be honest: it looks bad. U r down by 3 votes and debate was last chance to move needle. Also prob snow day tomorrow so even harder to reach voters

If James not in race, can we pick up votes from his supporters?

James had no supporters. Except Xander. Who hates you

There must be something we can do

I'm an evil genius, not a magician. Can't pull votes out of thin air. But I will keep thinking. In meantime, try to get Sophie to write another article

I will try. But she has been v annoying about helping me

I told you the media are vultures

CLAUDIA

Five minutes after that, the last—and definitely most horrible—major repercussion happened: Sophie and I got in a gigantic fight that was at least 17 times worse than the fight in Chapter 20.

It was so bad that when it ended, I was pretty sure my whole friendship with Sophie was over.

I really wish I was exaggerating.

had to use phone b/c Sophie can't use ClickChat on school nights (but CAN talk on phone) (which makes no sense) (but whatevs)

SOPHIE

So, you called up and started yelling at me for only writing about the squirrel.

And I was like, "That's all I wrote about, because that's all that HAPPENED."

Then you basically ordered me to write another article—

CLAUDIA

I didn't order you—

SOPHIE

That's how it sounded! And I told you I could only write another article if there was something to write about. I couldn't just write about nothing.

CLAUDIA

This was very frustrating. Because if you ask me, a couple of those Reese articles WERE about nothing.

And it just seemed crazy that the only way I could get ANY kind of coverage was by doing something totally insane, like murdering a bunch of avatars or letting an animal loose in school.

So I told Sophie she should write about my Big Sibling idea, because A) it was a great idea that'd totally improve life at Culvert Prep, and B) her articles hadn't mentioned it AT ALL.

SOPHIE

That really made me mad. Because I'm a reporter. I REPORT stuff. So if you don't talk about it, I can't report it.

And you'd hardly ever talked about the Big Sibling thing! So for you to suddenly be all, "Write this article about this thing I've NEVER EVEN DISCUSSED"?

It was crazy! So I said, "I'm not your puppet, okay?"

And then YOU said, "No kidding! You're Kalisha's puppet!"

CLAUDIA

Are you sure I said that? I could've sworn I was just thinking it.

WHAT I WAS THINKING:

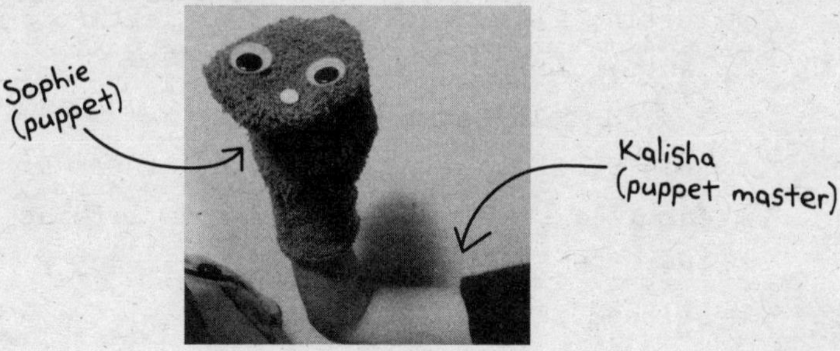
Sophie (puppet)
Kalisha (puppet master)

SOPHIE

You definitely said it. And it TOTALLY set me off. Because I am NOBODY'S puppet.

CLAUDIA

Sophie exploded. She was like, "Why don't you quit blaming me and take a look at yourself? You're all, 'Blah blah blah, Reese is so bad'—but you NEVER ONCE gave anybody a reason to vote for you!"

Which was incredibly hurtful. And seemed like total proof that Sophie was NOT on my side.

So I said—and I know this was drama-queen-y, but I was VERY upset—"I can't believe this! You actually WANT me to lose!"

SOPHIE

Which was RIDICULOUS!

CLAUDIA

I was mad! Then you started going on about how journalists have to be fair to everybody. Which just made me madder. So finally, I said, "What's more important to you: being a journalist, or being my friend?"

SOPHIE

And then I said, "What's more important to YOU: being president, or being MY friend?"

CLAUDIA

I said, "That's crazy! Why do I have to choose?" And THAT'S when you REALLY got mean.

SOPHIE

I definitely shouldn't have said what I said right then.

CLAUDIA

But you did. You went, "You're right—you don't have to choose. Because your campaign stinks so bad, YOU'RE GOING TO LOSE no matter what!"

WHAT MY FIGHT WITH SOPHIE WAS LIKE
(ok not really)
(but it FELT like this)

SOPHIE

And that's when you hung up on me.

CLAUDIA

I didn't hang up on you. YOU hung up on ME.

SOPHIE

No way! YOU hung up first.

CLAUDIA

Okay, whatever. Somebody hung up on somebody. Then Sophie called Carmen. And I started messaging Carmen and Parvati at the same time.

CARMEN

I'd never heard Sophie that upset. And you were so mad, you were typing in all caps for, like, an hour.

And I did NOT know what to do. Because you're both my friends! But you were trying to make me choose sides.

PARVATI

I'm just glad we had a snow day Thursday. 'Cause it would've been a NIGHTMARE trying to figure out who was going to sit with who at lunch. The drama level was just off the charts.

ESPECIALLY after you went nuclear, Claudia.

CLAUDIA

I am not proud of that. I should NOT have gone nuclear.

But I did: I unfriended Sophie on ClickChat.

CLICKCHAT NOTIFICATIONS PAGE FOR CLAUDIA TAPPER

You and sophie_k_nyc are no longer friends

CHAPTER 24 WORST SNOW DAY EVER

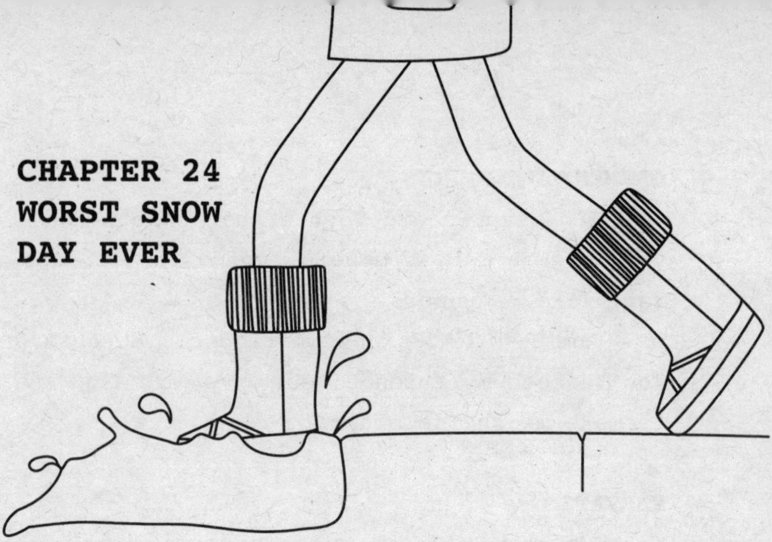

CLAUDIA

While I was going through an incredibly painful breakup with my best friend, Reese was getting back together with his.

REESE

Xander hadn't talked to me since Sunday. Which was REALLY bumming me out. Like, usually when he says he'll never forgive me and I'm dead to him? He gets over it in like an hour.

So this was pretty serious.

But that night, we were both in the same deathmatch on MetaWorld—and I saw this dude sneaking up on Xander.

So I snuck up on THAT dude and killed him. And Xander was psyched.

METAWORLD CHAT LOG

Skronkmonster killed Ghostrahm.
<<Skronkmonster: X i just saved u>>
<<XIzKillinIt: SWEET KILL>>
<<Skronkmonster: so r we cool now?>>
<<XIzKillinIt: I CANT STAY MAD AT U BRO...HUG IT OUT!!!>>

REESE

So we MetaWorld hugged. And I was like, "This is awesome—I should take a screenshot."

And that's how I wound up getting a shot of the EXACT moment Xander stabbed me in the back.

68401 MK / 22998807 GZ
00:17:44
Skronkmonster
XIzKillinit
strahm
Gho

METAWORLD CHAT LOG

XIzKillinIt killed Skronkmonster.
<<XIzKillinIt: PSICKE! I PWNED U!!>>
<<Skronkmonster: awwww no!>>
<<Skronkmonster: but r we cool now?>>
<<XIzKillinIt: NOT YET GOTTA SMACK YR CORPSE AROUND>>
<<XIzKillinIt: OK NOW WE COOL>>

REESE

So that was awesome. Then Kalisha texted me. And THAT was awesome, too.

KALISHA AND REESE (text messages)

You won the debate!

For realz????

Actually no. The squirrel won. But close enough! Check out the article: *http://culvertchron...*

Thats awesum!

transition = when new president comes in and old one leaves :(

Start planning your transition—YOU ARE GOING TO BE THE NEXT PRESIDENT OF THE SIXTH GRADE

WOOOOOOOOOOT!

Wait whats a transition

Notr Ar Realr Wordr

REESE

Then things got even awesomer! Because the next morning was a SNOW DAY! So me and Xander and Wyatt sledded Central Park! It was beast.

more sarcasm :(:(:(

CLAUDIA

I'm glad one of us was having fun.

I spent the rest of Wednesday night lying in bed, listening to Miranda Fleet breakup songs on repeat while I stared at my ceiling and wondered where I could move to start my life over.

supposedly about boyfriends—but lyrics actually made sense for regular friends, too

The next morning was even worse. Normally, I love snow days because Mom and Dad are at work and Ashley doesn't totally inappropriate for kids (but hilarious)

come in till three, so I can watch *Violent Housewives* without getting yelled at.

But that morning, watching it made me feel gross, because seeing the housewives go at each other just reminded me of my fight with Sophie. So I called Jens, figuring he would be supportive and cheer me up.

But that did not exactly work out.

JENS

You were so sad! And I wanted to make you feel better! This is why I said the Government of Students is stupid and no one cares about it. And you should let Reese be president and make something more cool with your life.

I was trying to help! I for sure did not think it would make you cry.

CLAUDIA

To be fair to Jens, once I started crying, he did take it all back. And he tried his best to comfort me.

Which I know was not easy. Because I was basically a hot mess.

But tbh, it made me worry about our relationship. Jens and I are very different people. And long term, I am not 100% sure it's going to work out.

The thought that I might have to break up with Jens—on top of my horrible breakup with Sophie—AND the fact that I was about to lose the election to someone who's so clueless he thinks "awesomer" is a word—was just too much.

I had never felt so sad and alone in my entire life. approx. 3x worse than when Meredith became a Fembot in 5th grade

So I decided to go to 16 Handles and eat my feelings.

Fortunately—because it is VERY unhealthy to eat your feelings, and frozen yogurt does not solve anything, even with unlimited toppings—16 Handles didn't open till eleven.

16 HANDLES
HANDLES
16
A

16 Handles (Upper West Side location)
(i.e., NOT Fembot hangout)
(also NOT open at 9:30am)
(should've called before walking over)

But after I'd walked all the way over there through the slushy streets, it did NOT seem fortunate. It just seemed like proof that my whole life was one big fail. So I trudged back home...and totally soaked my foot in a giant freezing puddle on Broadway and 79th.

That was pretty much the last straw. I cried the whole rest of the way home. When I got back to our building, I was such a puddle that Peter the doorman asked if he should call my parents. ← P is nicest doorman EVER

I went back up to our apartment, took off my soggy boots and socks, and got out my guitar. I'd been so busy with the campaign, I hadn't even practiced in almost a week. After I tuned it, I strummed some minor chords. ← minor chords = saddest of all chords

Then I decided to write a song about how miserable I was. But I'd only gotten one line written when Akash texted me with the shocking news: ← "It's over and it's dead/and I want to stay in bed..."—which tbh was kind of a lame line

AKASH (text message)

FEMBOT VOTE IN PLAY CALL ME ASAP

CHAPTER 25
THE FEMBOTS AWAKEN

(Zombie fembots rising from their graves)

CLAUDIA

Up until this point, I hadn't spent any time at all thinking about the Fembots, because A) they are not exactly huge fans of mine, and B) Akash had told me they never vote in elections.

But that hadn't stopped him from trying to cut a last-minute deal with them.

AKASH

Pretty much all the voters had made up their minds. And you were down by three votes. So the ONLY way you could win was if we convinced some NON-voters to vote for you.

And the only non-voters in the sixth grade are Fembots. So on Wednesday night, I messaged Athena Cohen.

And that's when I found out Reese had REALLY ticked them off.

AKASH AND ATHENA (ClickChat Direct Messenger)

Hey, AC—just checking in re. election. Any chance u might change yr mind about voting?

I told u voting is for losers

But I feel like I should just to make Reese suffer

That is FANTASTIC idea

Why shld Reese suffer?

OMG he is the WORST. He was SOOO cruel to Clarissa. And nobody messes w my friends. I AM GOING TO RUIN HIM

KALISHA

Okay, this part was crazy. REALLY crazy.

Remember how Clarissa was crushing on Reese? And I made him go to the yogurt place to hang out with her? But it was a train wreck, because he doesn't know how to talk to girls?

WHAT HAPPENS
WHEN REESE TRIES
TO TALK TO GIRLS
(not literally)
(it's a metaphor)

At some point during that whole thing... and I don't know if it was Reese's fault or Clarissa's...but she got the idea that they were ACTUALLY GOING OUT.

So Clarissa spent the next five days waiting for him to text her again. And getting REALLY mad when he didn't.

And because all the Fembots share the same brain, that got the rest of them worked up, too.

ATHENA

I'm sorry, but Reese was, like, TOTALLY classless. I mean, people break up all the time. They grow apart, they move on, whatever. It happens. No judgments.

But when you break up with somebody? HAVE THE DECENCY TO TELL THEM!

REESE

This is TOTALLY CRAY! I didn't even know we were going out! And if you're not going out with somebody? You should NOT have to break up with them.

CLAUDIA

I tried to interview Clarissa about the situation. But she wouldn't discuss it with me. All she'd say for the record were four words:

CLARISSA PARKER, Fembot/non-voter

I'm SO over it.

AKASH

Not by Wednesday night, she wasn't.

And I could've cared less about their little sixth-grade soap opera—except it gave us an opening big enough to drive a truckload of votes through.

ATHENA AND AKASH (ClickChat Direct Messenger)

I AM GOING TO RUIN HIM

Vote for Claudia! That would def ruin him

Yeah but irl who really cares about the election?

Reese does! Seriously, he'd be devastated if he lost. And if u and Clarissa/Meredith/Ling vote against him he will DEFINITELY lose

Maybe...But Claudia is totally lame.

Don't think of it as a vote for Claudia. Think of it as a vote AGAINST Reese

CLAUDIA

I'd just like to say that reading this made me uncomfortable.

AKASH

That's how most people vote! Why do

"negative ads" = campaign ads that make your opponent look bad

you think negative ads are so popular? Seriously, 99% of real elections come down to who voters hate less.

CLAUDIA

Just because it's true doesn't mean I have to like it.

And what came next made me even MORE uncomfortable.

ATHENA AND AKASH (ClickChat Direct Messenger)

If we vote for Claudia, what will she do for us?

What do you mean?

I know how politics works. My Dad gives major $$ to politicians. If I give Claudia votes, I have to get something for it

What do you want?

Give me a minute to think

AKASH

It took her a lot longer than a minute. It was more like two hours.

AKASH AND ATHENA (ClickChat Direct Messenger)

So....?

Hang on talking to Ling

OK here's what we need if u want our votes:

sushi in the cafeteria

cell phones in class

yogurt machine in lounge

Crème de la mer moisturizer in girls bathroom

TOTALLY CRAZY how expensive this stuff is (like $150 per ounce) winter break starts two days earlier

fire Ms. Santiago and Mr. Greenwald

no gym if you just got a manicure

$500

Let's take this offline. What's yr phone #

CLAUDIA

I have to say, I was personally shocked when I saw that list. If I'd known just how insane the Fembots' demands were, I NEVER would've agreed to a secret meeting with them.

AKASH

No kidding! That's why I didn't tell you about it until I'd bargained them down to one tiny, little, totally reasonable demand.

And give me some credit! I handed the whole election to you on a silver platter! All you had to do was show up for a meeting with the Fembots, agree to their one TOTALLY MINOR demand, and you'd win!

That's some A-plus evil geniusing right there. And you didn't even thank me for it.

CLAUDIA

Thank you.

I think.

CHAPTER 26
THE SECRET STARBUCKS SUMMIT MEETING

Shhhh...

CLAUDIA

My secret summit meeting with Athena and Meredith took place at the Starbucks on the corner of 85th and Lexington.

STARBUCKS AT 85TH & LEXINGTON AVE (major Fembot lair)
(when they want lattes instead of frozen yogurt)

STARBUCKS COFFEE

And because I had no idea what to expect—except that Akash had said the Fembots were offering to vote for me in exchange for some kind of political favor—I decided to wear a wire.

And by "wear a wire," I mean "keep my phone in my pocket with the voice memo app on."

Here's the transcript, minus a couple of minutes at the beginning when Athena made fun of Meredith for ordering a Gingerbread Chai Latte from the Secret Menu. And then told me my coat was "soooo retro."

Which I'm pretty sure is Fembot-speak for "ugly."

TRANSCRIPT OF SECRET FEMBOT SUMMIT MEETING

ATHENA COHEN: *I guess it looks good on YOU, though. I mean, as long as you're wearing that scarf, at least it matches.*

MEREDITH TIMMS: *Totally. It matches the scarf.*

ATHENA: *I just SAID that, Meredith.*

MEREDITH: *Sorry! I'm sorry.*

watching Meredith cower in fear of Athena was terrifying irl

CLAUDIA TAPPER: *So...Akash said you guys, um...*

ATHENA: *Right. So here's the deal: I can get you a ton of votes. Because, like, I don't want to sound egotistical? But my opinion matters. Like, people listen to me. So if I was, like, "Everybody vote for Claudia"—you'd win. No question.*

UGH! disgusting (but prob true)

MEREDITH: *It's totally true.*

ATHENA: *But, like, there's a price. Okay? Because, like, I'm sorry, but nothing's free. Okay? And, like, the sad thing is, there's SO LITTLE you can offer me. Because—ohmygosh, that boy over there is SO cute.*

MEREDITH: *He totally is.*

ATHENA: *Just look at him! I bet he goes to Collegiate.*

MEREDITH: *He is SO boss.*

ATHENA: *Settle down, Meredith! Ohmygosh, you're, like, drooling on yourself. It's sad.*

MEREDITH: *I wasn't! I was just—*

ATHENA: *Whatever. Control yourself.*

MEREDITH: *Sorry!*

CLAUDIA: *Um...so...*

ATHENA: *Okay. So, like, I talked to that Akash kid. And I'm sorry, but it is just sad how little power you have. I mean, it's, like, a total joke that you're, like, "president" or whatever. Because everything I asked for, he was, like, "Yeah...she can't actually do that." So whatever. But, like, this whole roof thing—like, that's under discussion, right? Like whether boys can play soccer up there and stuff?*

CLAUDIA: *There's been a lot of discussion, yeah.*

ATHENA: *And, like, people will actually listen to you? So if you go, "Here's what we should do with the roof," like, the principal or whoever will actually pay attention?*

CLAUDIA: *Well, I...yeah, I have a voice in it. Yeah.*

ATHENA: *So here's the deal: we want to sunbathe up there.*

CLAUDIA: *Sunbathe?*

FEMBOT SUNBATHING
(sorry, couldn't resist)

ATHENA: *Yeah. Like, not now. Obviously. But when it's warm. Like, May and June. Because the roof gets SERIOUSLY good light that time of year.*

MEREDITH: *Seriously. Really good light.*

ATHENA: *And it would be SO huge for laying down a base before summer. Like, if we could go up there during break and at lunch? And just get, like, twenty minutes to work on our tans? It would be SO boss. But, like, we can't have soccer balls flying all over the place while we're laying out. Or that—what was the thing that dork Carmen was talking about?*

MEREDITH: *Solar panels.*

ATHENA: *Ohmygosh. NO way. Because they'd just, like, get in the way and make shadows and stuff. So forget that.*

CLAUDIA: *But...umm...I mean, you can really only sunbathe up there a couple months a year? So—*

ATHENA: *The rest of the time, it should just be closed. Because you don't want people thinking they can just, like, go up there whenever they want.*

CLAUDIA: *I'm just a little worried that, um...it's kind of a tough sell? Because if I told, like, Vice Principal Bevan that I thought the roof should only be open for sunbathing? I'd probably get some side-eye for that.*

ATHENA: *DUH! Of course you would! That's why you have to lie. Like, make up a cover story. You wouldn't call it sunbathing—you'd call it, like, "quiet sitting" or, "enjoying the fresh air" or whatever. I mean, obviously. You don't call it what it is.*

FEMBOTS SITTING QUIETLY
(sorry again!)

MEREDITH: *Of course not.*

ATHENA: *So that's the deal—we make you president. And you give us the roof. For sunbathing. JUST us—like, keep all the soccer idiots and solar panel freaks and everybody else away from it. Okay?*

CLAUDIA: *Umm...let me just, like... talk to Akash. And make sure it's, uh... doable. And get back to you. Is that okay?*

ATHENA: *Whatever. Yeah. Like, if you don't want to win the election, that's fine, too.*

MEREDITH: *Totally fine.*

ATHENA: *Shut up, Meredith. I just said that.*

MEREDITH: *Sorry! Do you want a latte?*

CHAPTER 27
I GET ADVICE FROM GEORGE WASHINGTON

So here's what you do...
I'm listening...

CLAUDIA

The first thing I did when I left Starbucks was text Akash.

Actually, no. The first thing I did was drop my phone in a snowbank while TRYING to text Akash. Because I was freaking out. And running away from Starbucks as fast as I could. Through twelve inches of fresh snow. While wearing sneakers. couldn't wear boots b/c still soaked from earlier puddle

The second thing I did was find my phone in the snowbank. Then I had to dry it out on my sweater while praying it still worked. Which I guess counts as two things.

So really, the FIFTH thing I did was text Akash.

CLAUDIA AND AKASH (text messages)

SUNBATHING????!!!!!

It's a no-brainer

IT GOES AGAINST EVERYTHING I BELIEVE IN!!!!

Since when do you hate sunbathing?

I'M SERIOUS

Turn off the caps lock! It's like you're yelling in my ear

Sorry. But banning everybody from the roof all year...so the Fembots can sunbathe in June? It's SO wrong! I'm supposed to be a president for everybody!

You won't be a president for ANYBODY if you don't get re-elected

I prob can't get Mrs. Bevan to agree to it anyway

Then great! Say you'll do it, get their votes. After the election, tell them you tried and couldn't make it happen

So you want me to lie to them?

This self-righteous thing is really annoying, Claudia

Sometimes politics isn't pretty

You want to win? Make the deal

You want to lose? Don't make the deal

But don't get mad at me for doing my job

I'm sorry. And thank you. I know how hard you've worked for me, and I really appreciate it. You're a good friend. 🙂

You're welcome. Now quit texting me. I'm trying to play Blunt Force

CLAUDIA

I seriously did not know what to do. I was desperate for advice. But there was nobody around to give it to me.

I couldn't ask Carmen, because I knew she'd freak out about the Fembot-solar-panel situation. And Parvati was at Carmen's, so I couldn't text her without getting Carmen involved.

Mom and Dad were at work, so I couldn't talk to them.

Jens was on his way to a movie. And tbh, kind of terrible at giving advice. except about clothes (and soccer)

Ashley was probably at an audition. And also not great with advice. except about clothes (and makeup)

The person I REALLY wanted to talk to was Sophie...but we weren't friends anymore. INCREDIBLY SAD :-(

So I wound up talking to George Washington.

Not literally, because he has been dead for 200 years.

And I didn't PLAN to talk to him—I just sort of stumbled on him.

Here's what happened:

By the time I finished texting Akash, I was on the M79 heading back to the West

Side. And I wanted to go for a long walk, because long walks are a great way to clear your head and think about stuff.

Unfortunately, New York City after a snowstorm is a terrible place for long walks. Especially if you're wearing sneakers that are already half-soaked.

But the M79 stops right by the Met—and the Met is ENORMOUS. You can literally spend the whole day in there and not even see all the rooms.

So I decided to go to the Met and walk around until I could get my head straight.

THE MET (aka Metropolitan Museum of Art)

I started out in ancient Egypt, because Cleopatra was the most famous female leader I could think of, and I figured she might have had to deal with problems like the Fembots when she was queen. So if I could find her mummy or something, it might be very inspiring for me.

But it turns out Cleopatra did not leave a mummy. Or, tbh, anything else inspiring. At least not at the Met.

Then I left Egypt and got seriously lost. Plus the latte I'd had at Starbucks went straight through me. So pretty soon I was both seriously lost and REALLY had to pee.

Eventually, I found a bathroom. After that, I went back to just being seriously lost.

I was starting to think my whole "walking around the Met" plan was just the cherry on top of the Worst Snow Day Ever when I turned a corner and saw—from four rooms away—the most gigantic painting I've ever seen in my life.

It was called *Washington Crossing the Delaware*.

Washington crossing Delaware
tourist crossing Washington

And it showed George Washington kicking serious butt. 1st president/father of our country (duh)

I felt like finding that painting was some kind of sign. And I should sit there for a while and try to imagine what George Washington would tell me to do if he was A) still alive, B) willing to talk to me about sixth grade politics, and C) didn't get too confused when I tried to explain things like ClickChat to him.

It didn't take more than a minute of staring at that painting to figure out what George Washington's advice would be:

mostly b/c he was standing up in boat (and looked v. confident)

Stand up for what you believe in.

And this is what I believe: politics ISN'T about cutting shady deals, or lying about your opponents, or posing for stupid photo ops, or sucking up to reporters to get them to write good stories about you.

It's about trying your hardest to make life better for people—and not just people who can do you favors, but ALL the people you represent.

And I realized Sophie was right: the whole campaign, I hadn't talked about that AT ALL. I hadn't given people a reason to vote for me by standing up for what I believe in!

So I decided to write a manifesto.

DICTIONARY

manifesto

manifesto | man-ə'-fes-tō | noun
a public statement of goals, opinions, or objectives, usually political in nature

I whipped out my phone, right there in front of the George Washington painting, and typed out everything I should've said from the beginning.

Then I posted it on ClickChat. Because in the 21st century, if you are going to write a manifesto, ClickChat is the place for it.

CLICKCHAT POSTS ON "CLAUDAROO" (AKA CLAUDIA TAPPER) WALL

claudaroo

37 likes

claudaroo TO THE CULVERT PREP SIXTH GRADE: Before you vote in the election tomorrow, I want everybody to know where I stand on some important issues:

claudaroo FIRST, I believe a class president should represent EVERYONE fairly and equally. I think our school is awesome, and I want to make sure everybody, no matter who you are or what stuff you're into, has an equal chance to enjoy that awesomeness.

claudaroo SECOND, I am VERY sorry for the comments I made about soccer. I said them in a fit of anger during a fight with my brother, and I absolutely did NOT mean them. It's true I am not exactly a soccer fan, but I do NOT want to ban it. And as president, I would do my best to treat soccer players fairly and equally.

claudaroo THIRD, even though I am not a soccer fan, I think banning it from the roof was a mistake. Obviously, people should NOT kick soccer balls off the roof. BUT I think there must be ways to make sure that doesn't happen. If I get re-elected, I'll work with the administration to make rules about that.

claudaroo FOURTH, the roof is a place we should ALL be able to enjoy, no matter who we are. I think there must be a way to share it equally so kids can use it for sports, sunbathing, solar panels, and whatever else they want. Like I said, Culvert Prep should be awesome for ALL of us, no matter who we are.

claudaroo FIFTH, THANK YOU! Serving as your president for the past three terms has been a wonderful experience. And even though I think I would do a GREAT job in a fourth term, if you disagree and want to vote for someone else, that's ok, too.—Claudia

CLAUDIA

Right after I posted my manifesto, I sent Sophie a ClickChat friend request. Which was seriously embarrassing, because I never should've unfriended her in the first place. But fortunately, I didn't have to wait long for a response:

CLICKCHAT NOTIFICATIONS PAGE FOR CLAUDIA TAPPER

sophie_k_nyc has accepted your friend request

YAY!!!!!

CHAPTER 28
BEST SNOW DAY EVER

CLAUDIA

The rest of the snow day was pretty great. Sophie came over, and we hugged it out. Then we both promised never to fight like that again.

Then we made hot chocolate and watched *Thrones of Death*. Because Sophie's parents don't let her watch it at her place.

Technically, mine don't, either. But it was a snow day, so I figured the normal rules shouldn't apply.

NOTE TO MOM/ DAD: watching Thrones of Death did NOT scar me for life

After that, we baked some chocolate chip cookies. We'd just taken them out of the oven when Reese came back from sledding with Wyatt and Xander. And because we'd made way more cookies than we could eat, we gave them some.

Reese and his friends were actually fun

to hang out with for a change. Or at least they were until Xander put his wet socks on top of the oven next to the cookies.

cookies
(delicious)
Xander's socks
(COMPLETELY
DISGUSTING)
(also fire hazard)

REESE

Yeah, that was pretty gross. I told him not to do that.

WYATT

Sometimes, it's annoying being Xander's friend. He dropped a wet sock right on top of one of my cookies.

XANDER

Y'all were WAY too uptight about dem socks. But dem cookies doe! BEAST!

CLAUDIA

The best thing about the whole afternoon was that nobody mentioned the election. Personally, I felt like by posting my manifesto, I'd said everything I needed to say. And after a week of obsessing about it 24/7, I just wanted the whole thing to be over.

I think Reese felt the same way.

REESE

The thing about a snow day is, you shouldn't HAVE to think about stuff like elections. You should just have fun.

Like, at one point when we were sledding, Max Esper called and said we had to have a meeting about the transition. He was all, "Something something agenda, blah blah blah committees."

And I was like, "Dude, we can have a meeting—but ONLY if it's on an inner tube going down Cedar Hill."

And Max wasn't into that. So no meeting.

Cedar Hill—insanely crowded, but second-best sledding in Central Park (after Pilgrim Hill) (see Chapter 9)

CLAUDIA

After Sophie left around dinnertime, I finally went back on ClickChat to see how my manifesto was doing.

It had 37 likes. Which I thought was pretty good, considering I didn't pay for them. unlike SOME PEOPLE (Kalisha)

Although 37 votes wasn't enough to win the election. And some of the likes were from people in other grades. Plus camp friends. And my cousins. And at least one rando.

"rando" = random person who follows you, but you have no idea who they are (might actually be robot) (if they have 0 posts + 2 followers + follow 3,000 people)

So it was hard to tell if the manifesto had changed anybody's mind. And the comment Athena left under my post did not exactly make me feel great:

CLICKCHAT COMMENTS ON "CLAUDAROO" (AKA CLAUDIA TAPPER) WALL

Parvanana #VoteClaudia ☺ ☺ ☺ ☺

c_2_the_g V proud to be your running mate

kuypersjens Super!

goddessgurrl Good luck not being president, loser

ATHENA THE FEMBOT

CLAUDIA

(also every other night)

Mom and Dad both worked late that night, and I was already in bed when Mom got home. She came into my room to say goodnight, and I showed her my manifesto. Which she told me was awesome.

Then she gave me a little speech about how proud of me she was, and how much I had going for me brains- and talent-wise, and how no matter what happened in the election, there were a ton of ways I could make a difference in the world, so I shouldn't sweat it if I lost.

I felt very good about that...until

weeks later, when I interviewed Reese for this oral history and found out what Mom told him in HIS going-to-bed speech.

REESE

She was like, "Dude—YOU BETTER BE NICE TO YOUR SISTER if you win. Because this election's SUPER-important to her, and if she loses, she'll be CRUSHED. So don't do any sideline celebrating like when you score a goal in soccer. Or I'll take away your phone for a month."

CLAUDIA

I can't believe it. Mom didn't think I was going to win! SHE GAVE ME THE "LOSER" SPEECH!!!

Mom horrified at this—says we are "totally misrepresenting" her speeches

REESE

You think YOU got a bad speech? MOM DIDN'T TELL ME I HAVE BRAINS OR TALENT! It's like she thinks I'm a total slug who just sits around playing video games!

CLAUDIA

You kind of are, though.

REESE

I PLAY SOCCER! THIS FAMILY IS SO UNFAIR!

Reese getting too emotional agai

CLAUDIA

Mom wasn't the only one who didn't think I could pull it off. Right before I fell asleep, I got a ClickChat message from Akash:

AKASH AND CLAUDIA (ClickChat Direct Messenger)

Just saw yr manifesto. You actually WANT to lose, don't you?

What do you mean?

What did I tell you about flip-flopping?

All I did was tell the truth. And I feel really, really good about that.

Then I'm happy for you. As long as you realize you're doomed

CHAPTER 29
THE VOTERS VOTE

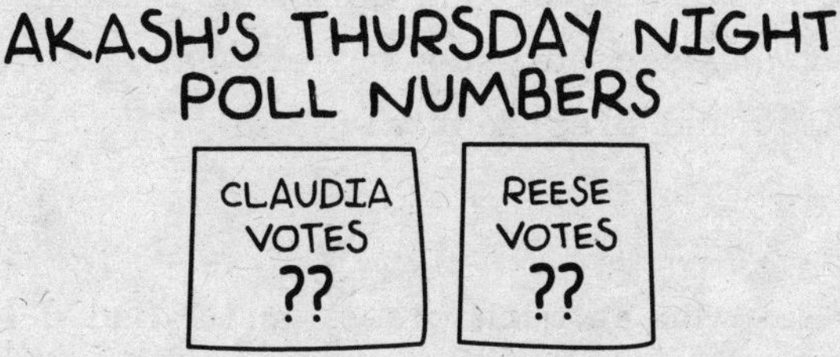
AKASH'S THURSDAY NIGHT POLL NUMBERS
CLAUDIA VOTES ??
REESE VOTES ??

CLAUDIA

No matter what everybody else thought, I did NOT believe I was doomed. I still had faith that the voters of the sixth grade would read my manifesto, realize I was the best person for the job, and re-elect me president.

But I was crazy nervous that whole day.

REESE

I can't believe you barfed up your breakfast.

CLAUDIA

I did NOT barf up my breakfast.

I ALMOST barfed up my breakfast. Also, I had to skip lunch. Because breakfast was still an issue at that point.

BTW, walking around thinking I might barf at any second made it very hard to look confident and presidential.

JENS

I saw you at math class, and I had a lot of worry. Because your face was gray-colored.

PARVATI

I remember at lunch, I was like, "OMG, Claude—are you going to pass out?"

CLAUDIA

It was a rough day. And it didn't exactly help that every time I passed my brother in the hallway, some soccer idiot was high-fiving him and yelling "YOU DA MAN!"

REESE

All the dudes on my team had my back. Which was beast! Except when Bryce said they were going to dump a cooler of Gatorade on my head when I won. I was a little worried about that. Gatorade's really sticky.

what Bryce was thinking
(NOT COOL to do this in school library)

CLAUDIA

The whole day, I kept hoping just one Reese voter would come up and tell me the manifesto had changed their mind. But nobody did.

So by the time Mrs. Bevan started handing out ballots at Friday Assembly, I was starting to think I might be doomed after all.

I was so stressed that when Xander jumped up and screamed "FREE J-MO!" I practically fell out of my chair.

SOPHIE

That was SO immature.

XANDER

Somebody had to represent fo' dat political prisoner, yo! FREE J-MO! FREE J-MO!

KALISHA

I hate to get all uptight—but when Xander tried to get people to chant "NO JUSTICE! NO PEACE!"? I felt like that was very insulting to actual victims of injustice.

James Mantolini wasn't even suspended that day. He just had to sit in the principal's office during Assembly so he wouldn't cause trouble.

JAMES

If you don't think Principal Spooner's office is a prison, you have CLEARLY not spent any time in there. It's like Alcatraz. If Alcatraz was full of ceramic cats.

Principal
Spooner's
office

CLAUDIA

After Mrs. Bevan sent Xander to join James in the principal's office, she started walking through the room with the ballot box. Each time somebody stuck a ballot in the box, I tried to guess who they voted for.

A lot of votes were totally obvious.

Sophie, Parvati, Carmen, Charlotte, Yun, Jens: me. if Jens didn't vote for me, our relationship was DEF OVER

Kalisha, Wyatt, Max, Bryce, Tucker, Dave: Reese.

Athena, Clarissa, Ling, Meredith, and all their wannabes: nobody.

Some votes were mostly obvious, like Charlotte (me) or Dimitri and Toby (Reese). And a couple were a tough call. But there wasn't a single likely Reese voter that I thought I'd definitely won over. As they put their ballots in the box, not one of them looked my way or smiled or gave me a thumbs-up.

So as Mrs. Bevan counted the votes, the shaky/gross feeling in my stomach got worse and worse.

And when she announced that Max had won the treasurer's race, it felt like a very bad sign. I reached out and gave Carmen's hand a squeeze and whispered "Sorry!"

CARMEN

I wasn't sad for ME that I lost. I was sad for Planet Earth.

CLAUDIA

As Carmen held my hand and whispered "Me too!" I realized I was going to lose.

So when Mrs. Bevan cleared her throat for the final announcement, and Sophie reached out to hold my free hand, I told myself it was okay...because our being friends again really WAS more important than my being president.

I also told myself I was NOT GOING TO CRY.

But then I started to cry anyway. I was halfway out of my seat to run for the girls' bathroom when Mrs. Bevan announced that I'd won.

PARVATI

OMG YOU WON! IT WAS THE GREATEST THING EVER!

SOPHIE

I was so excited for you! Like, I LITERALLY jumped up and down. 'Cause tbh? I was super-worried my articles might have cost you the election.

JENS

I was for sure proud of you by winning.

MAX

I couldn't believe it! I ran on the same ticket as a loser! What was I thinking?

BRYCE

I just wish I hadn't bought all that Gatorade.

KALISHA

I wanted to demand a recount. My polling was SOLID—Reese should've won by three votes!

But when I tried to get him and his soccer friends to chant "RECOUNT!"?

They were like, "Ehhh, forget it. Have a Gatorade."

REESE

It's not like I wasn't bummed that I lost. But it was two minutes till the weekend—so if there was a recount, we would've had to stay after school. And I just wanted to go to Wyatt's and play Xbox.

CLAUDIA

According to Mrs. Bevan, I won by one vote. Since the voting was anonymous, there's no way to tell who voted for who and/or whether my manifesto was what won it.

AKASH

It HAD to be the manifesto. My polling numbers matched Kalisha's—going into Thursday, you were DEFINITELY down by three votes.

So I guess it's okay to be a flip-flopper after all.

Which means I have to rethink everything I know about politics.

KALISHA

I've got to hand it to you, Claudia: this wasn't just a victory for you. It was a victory for your whole approach.

It turns out you actually CAN win an election by being honest and idealistic.

I'm still kind of shocked about that.

CLAUDIA

Thanks, Kalisha. And I'm glad that no matter how hard you tried to destroy me with totally unfair attacks on my character, we were able to get past all that and still sit at the same lunch table.

KALISHA

Well, I WAS pretty annoyed that Reese lost.

But I still got extra credit in social studies. So it's all good.

AKASH

Hey, Kalisha—did you know Film Forum's showing a revival of *All the President's Men*? It's a pretty cool movie. So...if you're not doing anything else this weekend...y'know...

FILM FORUM: best place in NYC to watch old/classic movies

FILM FORUM
1 GUEROS "EXUBERANTLY NOW" - SCOTT. TIMES
2 SATYAJIT RAY'S APU TRILOGY
3 IRIS/DIOR & I-BOTH END MAY 28
FILM
FORUM

KALISHA

Are you asking me out on a date?

AKASH

Not if you're going to get weird about it.

Kalisha and Akash are kinda-sorta going out now (which is cute) (although evil genius + evil genius = scary) (esp. if they ever have kids)

REESE

You know what? It kinda makes sense that I lost. It's like in soccer—the team that wants it the most usually gets the win.

And you DEFS wanted it the most.

CLAUDIA

So in the end, even though it got seriously ugly at times, the election wound up working out just fine for everybody.

Well, not quite everybody.

XANDER

WE WUZ ROBBED, YO! Straight up!

JAMES

Mark my words, Claudia: the revolution's coming.

Until then, my silent protest speaks for itself.

James's silent protest
(wore tape on mouth for 3 days)
(then Mrs. Bevan made him stop)
(which James said only proved his point)

EPILOGUE
(aka A BRIEF CONSPIRACY THEORY ABOUT THE ELECTION)

CLAUDIA

If the idea that I won the election by standing up for what I believe in makes you happy...and you are totally satisfied with how this history ended...stop reading right here.

NO, SERIOUSLY—STOP HERE

REESE

That IS the way it ended! You crushed it, Claudia! Hooray for you!

CLAUDIA

I'd like to believe that. I really would.

But a few weeks after the election, Student Government was debating my proposal for everybody to share the roof equally—which, BTW, wound up becoming official school policy, and I am very proud of that.

And during the debate in SG about the roof, Max was all up in my business. Because he'd suddenly decided he was TOTALLY AGAINST ANYBODY using the roof for ANYTHING except what he called "quiet sitting."

also, soccer got un-banned (but w/rule that nobody can kick balls off roof)

Which was very strange. Because the only other time I'd ever heard the term "quiet sitting" was when Athena used it during our secret Starbucks meeting.

And the day before the SG debate, I saw Max walking out of Starbucks with all four Fembots...holding what looked like a Gingerbread Chai Latte.

Claudia

GINGERBREAD CHAI LATTE

(from Starbucks Secret Menu)

(also Fembot Secret Bribe????)

I'm not saying the Fembots DEFINITELY bribed Max to get him to support their sunbathing on the roof idea.

I'm just saying it's possible.

MAX

That's ridiculous! I've ALWAYS been a huge supporter of "quiet sitting"! My position on the roof was a matter of conscience.

"matter of conscience" = what politicians say when they feel VERY strongly about something (OR ARE LYING)

CLAUDIA

Either way, Max and I were arguing about the roof. And I told him I had a mandate from the voters to make sure everybody shared the roof equally.

"mandate from the voters" = when you get elected to do a specific thing (like share the roof)

And Max yelled, "You don't have a mandate! Your brother lost on purpose!"

MAX

It's not like I can prove anything. But when we had that snow day, and I called Reese to set up a meeting about the transition? He told me meetings were lame, and he'd rather eat his own foot than go to one.

prob not exact quote (Reese usually says "eat my own HEAD")

So I said, "Reese—you realize being president is NOTHING BUT MEETINGS, right?"

He said, "Really?"

I said, "Really. It's all meetings. Plus speeches. Plus all the prep for the meetings and speeches. So you need to get to work."

Then Reese went, "Uhh...thanks for the heads up."

But the way he said it? It was like a light had just switched on in his brain. And he realized if he was president, he'd HATE EVERY SECOND OF IT.

REESE

No way! That's totally cray! I was ONE HUNDRED PERCENT into being president! Including the meetings! And the speeches!

I mean, maybe not 100%. But DEFINITELY 80%.

Or at least 50%.

KALISHA

Now that I think about it...I did get this weird text from Reese the day before the election.

REESE AND KALISHA (text messages)

What wld hapen if I dropped out of race?

I'd kick your butt into next week

Srsly?

Seriously. Your life would not be worth living. Why do you ask?

No reason its all good

KALISHA

I didn't really sweat it. Because Reese knew I was serious. If he'd tried to quit on me? After all the work I put into making him president?

I would've kicked his butt HARD.

I still would. I'm the kind of person who carries a grudge. And I'm four inches taller than Reese is. So I can take him.

REESE

This is cray! Seriously! I did

EVERYTHING Kalisha told me to! Right up until the end!

CLAUDIA

Really? Who'd you vote for?

REESE

Me! I voted for me! Of course I voted for me. Why wouldn't I?

What are you getting at here, Claudia?

CLAUDIA

Like Max said, I can't really prove anything. But here's my theory:

The day before the election...when Max told him about all the work he'd have to do once he got elected...Reese realized something.

HE DIDN'T ACTUALLY WANT TO BE PRESIDENT.

But he couldn't quit. Because if he did, Kalisha would kick his butt. So Reese was going to be stuck with a job he didn't want. And he'd be miserable.

EXCEPT...he was only winning by three votes.

So if he secretly voted for me—

REESE

A-ha! See! That's why your theory's cray—because I only have ONE vote!

So even if I voted for you, I'd still win by, like...okay, I forgot how to do the math here.

CLAUDIA

You'd win by one vote. Because if you were up by three and switched your vote, it'd be one LESS vote for you and one MORE vote for me.

REESE

Right! So EVEN IF I voted for you, I'd still win!

CLAUDIA

But if you got a SECOND person to switch their vote...then I'D win.

By one vote. Which is EXACTLY how many votes I won by.

REESE

But there's no way! Like, who could I even get to switch their vote from me to you and NOT tell Kalisha? It'd have to be a total secret!

CLAUDIA

Oh, sure. Huge secret.

The kind of secret that could only be kept by someone very close to you.

Like, say...

YOUR BEST FRIEND WYATT.

WYATT

Uh...no comment?

REESE

Dude! Don't say "no comment"!

WYATT

Why not?

REESE

'Cause it sounds bad!

And ballots are secret! Right, Claudia? Like, nobody can prove who voted for who?

CLAUDIA

Absolutely.

FIFTH
DISTRICT
3

SECRET BALLOT BOX (not actually used in 6th grade election) (ours was just cardboard box w/hole cut in top)

WYATT

Oh. Okay. Then no! Definitely no. I definitely did NOT vote for Reese.

I mean Claudia! I did NOT vote for Claudia!

I voted for Reese! Totally.

REESE

Me too! So your theory's TOTALLY CRAY, Claudia. There's NO WAY I secretly lost on purpose.

Please don't put it in the book. Seriously. Please?

CLAUDIA

I won't.

REESE

Thank you!

CLAUDIA

Unless I think it's important for future historians to know.

And/or I think you totally deserve to get your butt kicked by Kalisha for putting me through that whole nightmare of an election.

KALISHA

Reese, can I talk to you for a minute? Outside?

REESE

Oh, geez...

SORRY, REESE!

(not sorry)

SPECIAL THANKS

Liz Casal, John Hughes, Allegra Wertheim, Lucia Frank, Joe Newman-Getzler, Nick Spooner, Brittney Morello, Tal Rodkey, Alessandra Durstine, Jeeves The Dog, Isabel Mignone, Catherine Mignone, Rahm Rodkey, Ronin Rodkey, Nikhil Soltau, Michael Frank, Russ Busse, Andrea Spooner, and Josh Getzler.

ILLUSTRATION CREDITS

Liz Casal: pp. 1, 5, 11, 17, 24, 25, 33, 34, 41, 43, 49, 53, 57, 65, 73, 74, 83, 92, 93, 103, 109, 119, 129, 141, 142, 143, 149, 157, 158, 171, 178, 186, 192, 196, 208, 215, 224, 231, 242, 249, 253, 260
Nick Spooner: pp. 19, 20, 70
John Hughes: pp. 41, 138, 154, 155, 160, 162, 163, 166, 168, 172, 209
Tal Rodkey: p. 42
Joe Newman-Getzler: pp. 48, 81
Lucia Frank: p. 62
Allegra Wertheim: p. 66
Amanda Newman: p. 76
Dafna Sarnoff: p. 98

ABOUT THE AUTHOR

Geoff Rodkey is the author of the *New York Times* bestseller *The Tapper Twins Go to War (With Each Other)* and *The Tapper Twins Tear Up New York*, as well as the acclaimed adventure-comedy trilogy The Chronicles of Egg. He wrote the screenplays for the hit films *Daddy Day Care*, *RV*, and the Disney Channel's *Good Luck Charlie, It's Christmas*, and has also written for the educational video game *Where in the World Is Carmen Sandiego?*, the non-educational MTV series *Beavis and Butt-Head*, Comedy Central's *Politically Incorrect*, and at least two magazines that no longer exist.

Geoff currently lives in New York City with his wife and three sons, none of whom bear any resemblance whatsoever to the characters in *The Tapper Twins*.